AN AMISH DECISION

The Book of Eli and Ryan

Juliet Rohmer

In Search of Amish Love Series

Amish and Christian Romance

Amish and Christian Romance
An Imprint of Ordinary Matters Publishing
www.AmishChristianRomance.com

Book Layout © 2014 BookDesignTemplates.com

An Amish Decision / Juliet Rohmer. -- 1st ed. United States of America (December 2015)
ISBN-13: 978-1-941303-21-4
ISBN-10: 1941303218

Amish & Christian Romance
PO Box 430577
Houston, Texas 77243
www.AmishChristianRomance.com

Praise for AN AMISH DECISION

"*Lots of Amish adventure here. Just when you think you have it figured out, the author throws in another curve. Love the characters, especially Mattie. Although this is the first part of a series, it doesn't leave you on an annoying cliffhanger. . . . .*

This one's a keeper amidst a sea of Amish books that are maybes and just no's I've read in Amish Romance." ~ Theresa Lepiane, Amazon reviewer

"*One of the best Amish based books I have read. Down to earth and honest in emotion. A must read!*" ~ Devycat, Amazon reviewer

"*I loved this story! Couldn't put it down. I read the first one in the series, and it was enjoyable to read in this story how the two characters meet up again, and what transpired after so many years. Very good read.*" ~ Janis Ellwood, Amazon reviewer

Amish Romance by Juliet Rohmer

IN SEARCH OF AMISH LOVE SERIES

Visit and Like Juliet Rohmer's Facebook Fan Page:
Amish Romance Christian Inspirational Romance-Juliet Rohmer

A FREE Amish Romance for You!
For a limited time, you can get a free copy of the next Amish Rumspringa Romance. Sign up:

AmishChristianRomance.com

AN AMISH DECISION

THE BOOK OF ELI AND RYAN

It's been nearly fifteen years since Matilda King's rumspringa when she returned to her community to fully embrace the Amish life and married Samuel King. Now she's a widow with all the troubles that brings for a widowed Amish woman with four children and a farm. She's certainly not prepared for an old Englischer flame to step back into her life. More disruption follows as Matilda realizes she must make a major life-changing decision and wonders what impact will that have not only on her life but on those around her? She has, after all, been keeping a deep secret all this time.

Yet the Lord will command his
lovingkindness in the daytime,
And in the night his song shall be with me,
And my prayer unto the God of my life.

—PSALM 42:8 (KJV 1900)

CONTENTS

FOREWORD

Welcome to the Amish world of Matilda King and Ryan Meyers. The creation of this story has been a labor of love and a true delight. Like many, I find that the clutter of daily life can be overwhelming. The ability to lead a balanced life with God at the center can be a real challenge. Perhaps in response to my own inner desires, a simpler life where God is at the helm has bloomed and is peopled with Amish characters, pastoral landscapes, and a community culture.

I really enjoyed developing and learning about the story, the characters, and their struggles. After all, they're not so different from the rest of us outside of the Amish community. They dream dreams; they strive to reach goals; they struggle to reach Paradise, too.

I confess, Matilda King, Ryan Meyers, and their story fascinate me. Imagine having the love of your life reappear after so many years. What would you do? In *AN AMISH DECISION* you find out how Matilda King, Amish and now a widow, reacts to the reappearance of Ryan Meyers, an Englischer who is seeking God and has a real attraction to the Amish faith--and to Matilda.

Happy Reading!

Juliet Rohmer
December 01, 2015

CHAPTER ONE

The Sangre de Cristo Mountains were patched with fiery reds and vibrant yellows that made fire and the sun seem dull. Matilda King paused with a mug of hot *kaffe* in hand, turning in the field among the rows of potatoes and onions ready to be harvested. She took a brief moment to admire *Gott's* artwork that displayed itself on the mountainsides and bowed her head in reverence to it. Of all the seasons, she truly was in love with the fall, when the colors of the trees began to molt into different hues and filled the rugged terrain with vibrant colors.

Tears clouded her vision for a brief second. The fall had been Samuel's favorite season as well, and staring at the warm colors didn't feel right. Nothing felt right.

She turned back around and continued down the field to where Eli Lapp stood alongside her horses hitched to the potato plough and absently grazing on a few weeds that lingered. With the beginning shades of fall upon them, it also meant the start of their harvesting chores. Eli had suggested they start on harvesting now before a freeze came. He had little time to help her with the farm while caring for his own farm and job at a construction site he held an hour outside of Monte Vista. Furthermore, the

Farmer's Market was less than a week away, and her farm was in desperate need of repairs that required extra money that Matilda's paychecks couldn't cover. No matter how much she seemed to save, it was never enough.

Eli looked up from where he had been gazing studiously along the field, undoubtedly mapping the lines of potatoes from memory. Last spring he had helped her till the ground and plant various vegetables that grew easily in Colorado's weather; tomatoes, beans, potatoes, and onions were the easiest. However, unlike some of the neighboring *hauses* and barns, she also was able to get squash and cucumbers to grow in the unpredictable climate.

Gardening gave her a sense of ease and pleasure. There was nothing more relaxing than ripping weeds from the moist dirt and taking in a thriving garden free of them.

Wordlessly, Matilda handed the mug of *kaffe* over to Eli. His hazel eyes sparkled in the morning sunlight, and their hands briefly brushed. Calluses covered the expanse of Eli's fingers, typical of the Amish men who spent their whole lives out in the fields, and the center of her cheeks burned. She withdrew her hand, and buried it in the folds of her black dress.

"*Danka,*" Eli said, bowing his head.

He raised the mug and began to sip at the steaming liquid as he gazed out along the fields again. A strong hand reached up to tug at the edge of his dark beard that held the barest hints of grey. By Amish standards, Eli was handsome with his strong build and eyes that were a bit entrancing at times. His clothes, black trousers with suspenders, and a blue button up shirt, were tattered and patches roughly stitched on.

Eli's gruff voice brought her back from her observations, "It is a good day for harvesting."

"*Ya.* A very good day."

The morning sunlight bore down on her *kappa* and warmed the strands of her hair pinned smoothly underneath. She reached up to the string and adjusted it slightly as she shielded her eyes to find the shapes of her *kinner* in the distance.

Her eyes first settled on Rosella standing at the edge of the garden with a basket full of beans looped through her slender arm. Still young yet at *veertien*, she held a very authoritative and confident air as she supervised her younger *bruders* harvesting of the squash.

"Well," Eli said, handing the mug back to her, "we best get to starting if you want your vegetables for the winter. The afternoons may be warm, but a freeze is coming at night."

Matilda took the mug in one hand, careful not to let her hand touch Eli's again, and walked to the front of the potato plough. Habit borne of years working alongside her *daed* in the fields, and working the fields with Samuel, kicked in. She gathered the reigns connected to her horse's hitch and waited for Eli to grab the handles of the potato plough, pulling the depth lever down to pierce the dirt. He gave a brief nod and with a gentle cluck of her tongue they started forward.

As they walked along the rows of potatoes, Matilda kept a watchful eye over her *kinner* gathering vegetables in the garden and resisted the urge to turn around. The hair on the back of her neck stood on edge, an indication that Eli's eyes were resting on her as she walked the horses along.

Nine months.

Her heart contracted painfully at that, as it always did whenever her mind unconsciously counted the days since Samuel had died. Her loving and sweet *mann*. Seconds had turned to minutes, then hours, then days, then weeks, then months. It was unbearable at times watching time continue onwards even though her world had fallen apart within a matter of seconds.

Tears burned the surfaces of her eyes. Matilda blinked them away, careful to keep her head facing forward so not to alert Eli of her distress. A part of her scolded herself for hiding her grief from Eli who too had lost his *fraa* around the time she lost Samuel. If anything he knew of how much pain she was in.

Their friendship was a source of comfort, but over the past month or so Matilda had noticed a softening of Eli's eyes when he looked at her and a rare smile that graced his face. They were careful of their expressions, as they were taught from birth to control their emotions, and displays of affection were frowned upon; such things were meant to be private.

It was how Matilda suspected that Eli, during their course of friendship, had possibly developed romantic feelings for her. They were both near the end of their mourning periods, and as widows were allowed to remarry in the Amish community. It would be a *gut* and logical match with Eli. He had *kinner* of his own that needed a *maemm*, and she needed a *mann* to help around the farm. Both were doing a *fraa's* and *mann's* chores and it left them exhausted at the end of the day.

Except Matilda couldn't bear the thought of remarrying after Samuel. It didn't feel right, loving another man and in a way replacing Samuel's presence that lingered around the *haus* and life they built together.

They came to the end of the row. Matilda carefully guided their horses around and heard the clinks of rocks against the plough as Eli pulled the lever down again. She stared down at the several brown mounds that were now sitting above the surface, still wet from last night's watering. She prayed silently to *Gott* in thanks for the plentiful harvest that would feed her and her *kinner* during the winter.

The rest of the morning passed in silence that was occasionally punctuated with childish laughter from Matilda's *kinner* and Eli's attempts to make conversation. They were both reserved people, preferring quiet and only speaking when it was proper.

"*Maemm*! Look! Look what I have!"

Matilda turned at the sound of her son's voice. Isaac, a striking image of Samuel with his dark hair and piercing eyes, jogged to them with a pleased grin on his face. He held out a tiny arm and airily showed her the garden snake he held by the end of its tail.

The basket of potatoes fell from Matilda's arms as she stared, horrified, at the writhing snake in her son's grasp.

"Put that down, Isaac!" Matilda commanded. "Put it down now before it bites you."

Isaac looked up at her through his dark, curled lashes. A mischievous glint, the same one Samuel had right before he would steal a kiss or tickle her, filled Isaac's eyes. The glint had little to do with being affectionate.

"It's just a little garden snake, *maemm*. Are you afraid of one of *Gott's* creatures?"

He thrust the writhing creature towards Matilda who slapped his hand away in a pulse of fear and a little bit of amusement. The past few months had been hard on her *kinner* and they were slowly but surely starting to have a spark of childish humor in them again. She tried to keep her face neutral and stern as possible while gazing at him. In these light hearted moments, Matilda gave thanks to *Gott* for blessing her with *kinner* who could keep her smiling.

"No, I don't. Put it down," she said.

Isaac went to brandish it again at her, but Eli's voice cut through the warming air. "You heard your *maemm*, Isaac. Put it down. Now."

A defiant scowl started its way across Isaac's tanned face. Five years younger than Rosella, he had a bit of a stubborn streak that came from Samuel. Since his *daed's* death, Matilda had a hard time teaching him humbleness and that confrontations were not a part of their faith.

Fearing an argument that would undoubtedly ensue, Matilda straightened the black hat that was perched on Isaac's head.

"Everything is fine, Eli." She said, tightly. "Go on Isaac. Put it down and help your siblings bring in the vegetables. How about I make us some lunch?"

Isaac nodded before dropping the snake to the ground. He glanced at Eli, who stood a few feet away brushing a potato, before stomping back down the field to help Rosella and Matthew with what they harvested from the garden.

"I did not mean to interfere." Eli said, bowing his head when Matilda cut him a look. "It's a habit, to parent. You know how it is when you see a child misbehave."

Matilda sucked in a calming breath. As big as it was for Eli to apologize, something that did not occur regularly as the *mansleit* were generally right in their community, irritation stirred in her for having another man that wasn't Samuel reprimand her child.

"All is forgiven. Let's gather the rest of the potatoes and I'll make you lunch."

"You do not have to."

"Consider it my gratitude for all your help these past couple of months."

There it was again. The subtle softening of Eli's hazel eyes, a color that reminded Matilda of hay swaying in a late fall breeze.

"You've helped me, too, Matilda," he said.

The corner of his lips curled up into the barest trace of a smile. They quickly gathered the rest of the potatoes and let the horses graze in the pasture next to the field. While storing the potatoes in run sacks and hanging them on hooks in the little storage area of the barn, Eli turned to her.

"Have you thought of taking some of your vegetables and bringing them to the Farmers Market?"

Matilda shook her head. "*Nee*," she said, lifting a bag of potatoes onto a hook, "I don't have the time to spare. Between my *maemm's* bakery, the *haus*, the farm..."

A wave of exhaustion crashed on her just thinking of all the chores she had to do. She had been lucky that her *shtamm* and compassionate community were willing to help her enough through her grieving period by supplying food, watching her *kinner*, and whatever else that needed to be done.

Eli smiled sympathetically. He took the last bag of potatoes and hooked it before closing the door.

"I understand. I just thought since you have plenty of food from the harvest to get through the winter that selling it would help."

She paused in consideration at that. Not only had Samuel's death been a sharp twist to her gut emotionally, but it was a financial blow as well. The community didn't participate in the Englischers's world, but they still had to follow the laws. The upkeep and taxes were due soon. Samuel's earnings and her own paycheck had barely been enough to cover the taxes and repairs around the farm. They had harvested enough to keep themselves healthy throughout the winter, and relied on what little bit of money they had left over for other needed items. Now, it wasn't enough to prepare herself for the winter season, and the fences were in bad need of repair or else her cows would find a way to roam free out into the wilderness.

"Okay," Matilda said, nodding her head. "I can spare a few things and bake a couple extra pies. I'm sure my maem wouldn't mind if I used the bakery."

"*Wunderbaar.*"

They walked side by side to the back porch of the *haus*. Inside, the chatter of her *kinner* washed over Matilda soothingly. Her hand extended towards the screen door when it was stopped by the gentle force of Eli's fingers wrapped around her wrist.

"Matilda, I-I-" He swallowed thickly, shifting nervously foot to foot. "I need to ask you something."

Matilda's heart hammered in trepidation. At that moment she wished that Rosella or one of her kinner would appear and break the awkward tension that fell upon the back porch.

"I've been thinking about, you know, possibly remarrying later."

"That's *gut*, Eli. I know Katie would want you to move on." She said, swallowing thickly against the dread lodging in her throat.

"Right, but I've been thinking that I could possibly remarry to—well—to you."

He stammered the last part out. The center of Eli's cheeks, right above his beard line, flushed a deep hue.

A long pause followed as Matilda tried to formulate a good answer while reprimanding herself for forging a friendship with Eli. It was bound to happen, his feelings towards her. They were both recently widowed and the only two close to each other in age. She truly wanted to feel some sort of romantic stirring for Eli, but all she felt was a sisterly affection and care.

Not like in the past. Not like with Samuel where she had grown to passionately love him.

Eli's eyes shimmered at her as his fingers absently adjusted the rim of his black hat.

"I promise to think about it," Matilda said. "Right now, I think it's better that we remain the way are until we both feel certain we are ready to marry."

"I am ready to marry, though," Eli insisted quietly. Mindful of her *kinner* that could appear any moment, he tugged Matilda forward slightly and rested her hand on his beating heart. "I've grown to care about you, Matilda. About you, and your *kinner.*"

Matilda's heart ached at the confession. Grief brought everyone closer. She had learned that after Samuel's funeral, but it led Eli to think that she could possibly return his affections. She gently pulled her hand away from Eli's strong chest and reached up to cup his jaw through the bristles of his beard.

"You still love Katie, Eli. I know that you do. I still love Samuel. I just don't see marriage as a good move for us both right now."

"But in time, perhaps?"

She folded at the soft question. "In time, maybe. I'll think about it."

A small smile found its way to Eli's weather beaten face. He nodded his head before they took a step back and entered the kitchen to help Matilda's *kinner* finish storing the vegetables. As she worked and half-listened to Rosella chat to her about sewing a new dress to wear, Matilda began to silently pray for guidance and strength.

The last thing she would ever want to do was lose Eli, but losing Samuel's memory felt more lonely and painful.

The following Monday after walking her *kinner* to the schoolhouse, Matilda walked briskly along the sidewalks to her *maemm's* bakery. The occasional roar of the car of an Englischer driving by would punctuate the calm silence of the small town. It was still too early for Englischers to be filling the sidewalks or the businesses, but Matilda's day had started at five a.m. with morning prayers, and starting breakfast for her kinner.

She had to look as exhausted as she felt. When she splashed water on her face, her fingertips had felt the small tight lines at the corner of her eyes from lack of sleep and the early morning start. Matilda blinked a couple of times to rid the feeling as she reached the white building of Rebecca's Bakery. The last thing she had any patience for was hearing her *maemm's* fretting. Not after a sleepless night thinking about Eli's proposal.

There was a flurry of movement in the tidy and meticulously organized kitchen when Matilda stepped in through the back door. A wave of heat from the ovens and the smell of baking bread greeted her as she deftly unbuttoned her wool coat to hang it on a peg near the door. Her *maemm*, Rebecca, stood behind a counter rolling out a pie crust. Specks of flour dusted the skirts of her dress, a darker shade of blue. It was custom to see the older Amish women wear darker colors as a sign of their age. Despite the plain and light-colored dresses in her own closet, Matilda still wore the color of mourning.

Rebecca hummed quietly to herself a hymn they often sang at church, and placed the perfectly rolled pie crust into a pie pan. She turned to dust her fingers on the small pile of flour on the little island behind her and jumped at the sight of Matilda.

"Ach! Matilda! Don't go sneaking up on me, now. You gave me quite the fright."

"Sorry, Mama. I didn't mean to startle you."

She easily slid up to Rebecca's side and gave her an apologetic hug. Over the years, Matilda had begun to notice her *maemm's* petite frame grow more thin until it felt like nothing but bones underneath her pale and freckled skin. The stress of owning the bakery and trying to maintain the farm was beginning to wear them down. Especially since Samuel who had been young and hearty, had helped them out whenever he could. It was understandable why Rebecca had recently started encouraging her to accept someone like Eli. He was just as young, and strong.

"All is *gut*." Rebecca said, patting her fondly on the back. "Come. We have an hour before the store opens. I have breads baking and the pies need to be filled."

Matilda rolled up the sleeves of her dress before grabbing the nearest bowl of strawberry filling. The sweet smell of strawberries and sugar filled her nose pleasantly as she scraped the bowl clean with a spoon and into the already baked pie crust lined with cream cheese. The local Englischers were fond of their pies and the strawberry pie seemed to be the favorite. They baked several of them a day thanks to the bountiful season of harvested strawberries.

"How were your harvesting chores?" Rebecca asked. "I do hope that you have enough to get through the winter."

"More than enough. I have enough vegetables to sell to the Farmer's Market this weekend."

"*Gut*. I worry about you and my *kins-kind* getting enough to eat. You look like nothing but a bag of bones, Matilda."

The urge to point out that her *maemm* was nothing but bones as well flashed through her. Instead, Matilda distracted herself by wrapping the pie in plastic cellophane and placed it in the counter next to the other variety of pies.

"I'm fine, Mama. Now that the warm weather and harvesting chores are over I won't be outside continually."

"*Gut, gut.* I do hope that Eli will help you chop firewood to keep warm."

A pink hue filled Matilda's cheeks, and she turned around to grab a clean bowl to hide her embarrassment. It wasn't a secret to their community that Matilda and Eli were both recently widowed and near in age. Such things were not talked about, but Rebecca seemed to take it upon herself to find every excuse to push Matilda to Eli.

"Such a wonderful gentleman." Rebecca continued on, still smiling. "He offered to help us out around the farm, did you know?"

Hot anger pulsated through Matilda so strongly that she curled her fingers into clenched fists to keep herself from speaking out harshly. Anger towards Eli for trying to her parent her *kinner*, for offering to help her family, for her *maemm* who wouldn't stop talking about Eli and marriage, for *Gott* deciding it was time to take Samuel, the pressure to take care of her family; all of it swirled within her like a violent summer storm that sometimes graced the Colorado's skies.

She set the bowl down on the counter with more force than necessary, and the sound of the glass slapping the counter brought her back. As quick as it started, it faded away to shame. Matilda bowed her head and prayed for forgiveness for having such angry thoughts. She should be grateful for Eli's help and care for not only her, but for the rest of her family. Who was she to question *Gott's* decision to bring Samuel to Heaven even when he was so young and had a loving family? Things of that nature weren't known.

"Matilda?"

She looked up at Rebecca's startled voice and instantly flushed even darker in guilt at her *maemm's* wide eyes.

"I'm sorry. I-I-I don't know what's wrong with me today," Matilda said, sighing heavily as she smiled apologetically at Rebecca. "Maybe I am little more tired and grumpy than I thought."

"You obviously are." Rebecca stated, plainly. She arched a fair eyebrow at her. "Are you resting enough at night or having bad dreams again?"

"*Ja.*"

An awkward silence fell.

Certain topics were never discussed openly and the source of Matilda's dreams was one of those topics that wasn't meant for anyone else's ears.

"Have you talked to the bishop about the dreams? He could provide you with good advice and prayer." Rebecca said.

The last time Matilda had spoken with Bishop Abraham was during Samuel's funeral. She still remembered his age-spotted and rough hand rubbing circles on her shoulder as he reminded her that death was a blessing and that Samuel had gone to Heaven to be with their Lord. His words did little to comfort her then, and she doubted whatever words he spoke now would either. Doubts clouded her mind again and filled her with shame for her faithlessness.

Matilda smiled to appease her *maemm*. "Maybe I will. They're just dreams, Mama. I'm sure they'll stop in time."

"If you're sure. Grief does hard things to the heart and mind."

"I know."

A gentle tapping on the back kitchen door interrupted the conversation. Rebecca frowned, wiping her hands clean on her apron and hurried to the door.

"Morning, ma'am. I was wondering if I could talk to Matilda for a moment."

Eli's gruff voice echoed in the quiet and warm kitchen. She froze while scooping out a cup of sugar to add to the peaches that Rebecca had sliced for a pie. An indescribable emotion gnawed on the pit of her stomach.

"Of course. Matilda," Her *maemm* turned to look at her, "Eli is here to talk to you."

Matilda didn't move at first besides pouring the cup of sugar on the peaches. At the look of warning gathering in Rebecca's eyes, she dropped the measuring cup in the bag of sugar and went to the door.

"Morning," Eli greeted her, offering a small smile. He took a step back to put the proper amount of space between them. "I was wondering if we could talk for a moment..."

About last night, Matilda supplied, though he didn't say it out loud. She nodded and brushed by Rebecca, ignoring the smile on her face. They walked to the other side of the parking lot and out of ear shot.

"I wanted to apologize about being forward last night," Eli said, rubbing the back of his neck. "It wasn't very gentlemanly or proper of me to push marriage onto you. I know how hard it is to lose someone and feel like you are replacing them."

Matilda smiled thinly. "*Ja*. Eli—" She held up her hand when he opened his mouth, "I want you to know that I do care about you, but right now it feels too soon. To me, at least."

"I know. It probably is a bit rushed. I've just grown to care for you and your *kinner*. I can wait until you feel ready."

She sighed inwardly in exasperation at the immediate response. It wasn't just replacing Samuel with another *mann* that slowed her possible feelings for Eli. It felt like a betrayal to Samuel and their vows of love.

As Eli continued to talk, her thoughts wandered back to the summer where all of it had started. Rumspringa had begun for Matilda when she turned sixteen and like any other teenager in their Amish community, she had been a bit eager but also a little hesitant to experience the Englischers's world before deciding to join the church. Rebecca had encouraged her to go with Lucy to understand at the very least what she had within their tight-knit Amish community. Those months had been filled with make-up, perfume, English clothes that bared her skin, alcohol, books, and a boy named Ryan. Just thinking about the honey blonde hair that had felt like silk between her fingers and feeling soft, but supple lips pressing warmly against hers still brought hot shivers to her spine.

She had been wicked then and sometimes wondered if her decisions back then were returning to haunt her or were the reasons why she had always dimly felt a pang of resentment towards her *maemm*.

Her eyes drifted closed as Ryan's sapphire eyes flashed in front of hers like it was him standing in front of her, not Eli. She didn't have to visit the memory of him to remember those eyes.

They were the same as Rosella's.

CHAPTER TWO

The strands of Rosella's hair were soft around Matilda's fingers as she combed through the honey blonde locks. She gently gathered them and twisted them into a knot, careful not to pull it too tight, and pinned it into place before setting her white *kapp* on top. She soaked in their quiet mornings, and the smell of Rosella's freshly washed hair.

Rosella twisted around in her chair and grinned up at her, revealing a set of white teeth that were bucked out a little from years of sucking her thumb. While Matilda found the sight endearing, so uniquely her, Rosella thought the opposite as she entered her teens. It wasn't until Samuel had insisted that *Gott* and he found her beautiful, buck teeth and all, that Rosella embraced the feature.

A wistful smile crossed Matilda's face at the memory. She ran an affectionate hand down the curve of Rosella's neck and then patted her on the back. "You are ready to for the day. Come, let's make sure your *bruders* are ready to go."

Gathering her *kinner* went surprisingly easily despite how late they were already running. Their mornings were often chaotic with Isaac and Matthew darting around in endless energy that Matilda dearly wished she possessed. It was during those times that she missed Samuel's soothing presence. Cooperative, the two boys put their hats on over their dark hair without a fuss and carefully carried the pies Matilda spent the previous night baking to their buggy under Rosella's supervision.

Over the clopping of horse hooves on the ground, Matilda prayed that the day would be successful. Just yesterday Isaac had complained that none of his trousers fit right, and they wouldn't keep him warm during the winter. All the fabric Matilda had stored over the years for sewing was now empty with her *kinner* constantly growing.

They arrived to the Farmers Market a half hour later. Tents were propped everywhere in an outline of a large square and crowds of Englischers were already gathering. She spotted her *maemm* and *daed* standing beneath a large white tent to help shade them from the glaring sun. At night the air was frosty, but during the day there was still enough light and heat to burn.

Rebecca spotted them immediately and waved cheerfully in their direction. They returned the wave and quickly gathered their items from the buggy with her *daed's* help.

"Running a little late aren't we, now?" Jonathan said.

Two sacks of potatoes were perched easily on his broad shoulders. Even approaching his sixties, her *daed* was still incredibly fit from years of farm work. The only difference now was the protruding stomach that strained through his blue button-up shirt. She couldn't remember when the grey streaks in his brown beard had appeared, but age crept up on all of them. Matilda felt as if she had aged at least ten years in the past nine months.

"It was your *kins-kind's* fault." Matilda said.

Her *daed* turned around, bags of potatoes still perched on his shoulders to mock frown at them. "Is that true?

Your *maemm* better be lying or else there won't be any cookies left for you two boys to have."

The horrified expressions on Matthew and Isaac's faces filled Matilda with genuine laughter. She set a soothing hand on Matthew's trembling shoulder. "Your Papa is kidding. Come along now. Set those pies over there with the other ones."

She cast a glance around the market place in search of Lily, her younger *shveeshtah*, before turning to look at Jonathan in confusion.

"Where is Lily? I thought she was supposed to help us."

Jonathan shrugged his shoulders, potatoes ruffling in the bag. "She is around somewhere I'm sure. You know your sister. She can't ever hold still for more than a minute."

He left Matilda to unhitch the buggy and let her horses roam in the field the town let them use with the other horses behind the market. Before she joined her parents, a troubling sight caught her attention. Across the field near an oak tree, Lily's petite frame stood close to a boy Matilda recognized as Jacob Lapp. Their hands were clasped loosely between their bodies, and heads bowed close as they talked.

Matilda sighed in exasperation. Her sister's sixteenth birthday was approaching in a few weeks and that meant the start of courting and rumspringa. For a few months, Lily would experience the English lifestyle, something she clearly was eager to start from the sound of her flirty giggle that floated across the field.

She turned around to give them privacy, something they were taught to do whenever there was a public display of affection between couples, and folded her hands over the spot where her stomach muscles had tightened. Matilda closed her eyes at the onslaught of emotions streaming through her. Seeing her younger sister so happy to start courting and enjoy her *rumspringa* brought back the memories she had carefully stored away for the sake of her own sanity.

Matilda breathed in deeply, the smell of dry grass and dirt tickling her lungs. She started towards the tables that were set up earlier to help her parents and would talk with Lily later; to at least warn her on what could happen.

Gott knew that she had personal experience in that area.

A few hours later the strawberry and peach pies were gone along with Rebecca's canned raspberry preserves. Even Matilda's harvested squash and cucumbers disappeared quickly as the afternoon ticked by in a surreal haze of Englischers gracing the front of their table. Rebecca quickly counted the change, and they both sighed in relief. There was more than enough to repair the fence and a few other things around the farm.

Matilda stood behind the table with her hands folded neatly in front of her as Englischers passed by, and she returned their smiling friendly greeting. She kept one eye carefully trained on her *kinner* who had long since grown bored of staying behind the table and were darting around to visit with other members of the community.

She watched as Rosella walked up to a tall Englischer man with similar blonde locks as hers and began to chat with him, a smile curving up her lips. Matilda tensed slightly, inwardly scolding her daughter's confidence in talking to strangers. It was a trait she noticed from the first day Rosella learned to talk. Unlike her siblings or her parents, Rosella had more confidence in her abilities to talk to people. Most of the time she talked her *bruders* into doing her chores or talked her way out of punishment.

The only person immune to it anymore was Matilda.

She started forward to disengage Rosella from the Englischer, but Lily sidled up next to Rosella and placed a protective arm around her niece's shoulders. Matilda let out a relieved breath and went to turn away when the man suddenly turned to look at whatever Lily was pointing to.

Her breath hitched within her throat at the sight of sapphire eyes, so much alike Rosella's, and blonde hair slicked backwards to reveal a sharp face. A flash of heat curled at the base of her spine, and she stumbled into the table, stomach tightening into a million knots of dread. It couldn't be possible, no, it wasn't possible. The Englischer only dressed and looked like Ryan from his strong figure dressed casually in a pair of jeans and a white tee-shirt. Besides, he had no idea she lived in Monte Vista now since the last time they had seen each other she still lived in Lancaster and was only visiting Denver with her best friend Lucy.

"Matilda, are you all right?"

Rebecca was at her side in an instant, sweeping a fretting hand across the curve of her cheek to feel the heat there. Waving her *maemm's* concern away, Matilda forced an assuring smile on her face.

"*Ja*, Mama. I'm fine. It's probably just the heat."

Her *maemm* didn't let it go. Rebecca grabbed the metal box filled with their earnings and pulled out a ten dollar bill. "Here," she said, sliding it into Matilda's sweaty palm, "Take this and buy yourself a bottled water from the general store down the road. Take Lily with you to make sure you don't faint."

Matilda paled further at the thought of interrupting Lily's conversation with the handsome Englischer that looked so eerily like Ryan.

"That's okay, *maemm*. I can do it myself. Lily's busy."

Rebecca's eyes focused somewhere over her shoulder and a frown marred her features. "Nee she isn't."

Risking a glance over her shoulder, she let out a relieved breath to see that Lily now stood alone with Rosella. When she turned back around Rebecca's eyes were studying her intently. It was the same gaze that all Rebecca's *kinner* were familiar with; the one that said, "I know you are up to something and I will find out." Even as a fully grown woman she still shrunk back from it and hurried towards Lily.

"Rosella, can you please go to the tent with your *grohsmammi*? Lily and I have to go to the store."

Lily frowned at her. "We do?"

"Just do it, please." Matilda snapped without meaning to. At Rosella's eyes widening, she back-peddled hastily. "I mean, *ja*. We have to go to the store. I'm feeling a bit faint. I'll get you something from the store to share with your *bruders*, Rosella. It was the Snickers bar right?"

Rosella's face brightened at the prospect of having a candy bar. It was one of her favorite Englischer candies. She'd always had such a sweet tooth.

"The one with the caramel and peanuts?"

"*Ja.* That one."

"*Danka*, Mama."

When Matilda straightened, Lily had a suspicious look as she stared at her sister. Matilda tensed at the strange expression.

"What?"

"You just look really pale and panicked."

"It's the heat."

"Right, the heat."

The two sisters squeezed their way out of the Farmer's Market and took a quiet street to the general store. Matilda fanned herself with her hand, willing her body and emotions to calm down from the dread and fear shooting through her.

All of her efforts to calm herself vanished, however, when Lily turned to look at her and asked in a causal tone,

"So, how do you know the Englischer named Ryan?"

Matilda blinked once, twice. Unsure if she heard correctly or not and praying that she did hear incorrectly. She cleared her throat against the sudden onslaught of dryness coating it.

"I'm sorry. I-I didn't hear what you said."

They paused on the corner. Traffic roared by as they waited for the light to turn red so they could cross over to the grocery store located directly across from them. Matilda braced herself as she watched Lily study her face carefully, searching for something.

"There was an Englischer named Ryan who said he knew you from a few years ago," Lily said, finally.

Matilda's heart pounded so hard that she feared it would surely seize and stop beating altogether. Images of the tall blonde man who looked so eerily familiar flashed forward.

Ryan Myers. It had been him.

Matilda folded her hands over where the muscles lining the wall her stomach tightened again. Desperate to keep her composure and not draw more attention from Lily, she watched the traffic streaming by them in a blur of color and sound from the passing cars.

"Do you know him?" Lily pressed again.

The light changed, turned to green, and spared her from answering. Matilda moved forward with an unsteady gait alongside Lily down the crosswalk to the other side of the street. She kept her eyes forward and face neutral as possible as they entered the grocery store. After they paid for a Snickers candy bar for Rosella and a couple of water bottles, they made their way back to the Farmers Market.

Lily stopped and turned to Matilda in frustration. "So, are you going to answer my question or not? Do you know him?"

Matilda sighed. She twisted the blue cap of her water bottle with more force than necessary and gulped down a painful amount of crisp water.

"Does it really matter if I do or don't?"

"*Ja.* It does because he told me that he knew you and even looked for you back in Lancaster a few weeks ago."

Matilda paused in mid-step and nearly lost her balance. She looked over at her sister in surprise.

"He looked for me in Lancaster?"

Lily straightened, a glint of triumph showing in her eyes. "I knew it! You do know him."

Dread curled in the pit of Matilda's stomach. If Ryan had looked for her in Lancaster, which undoubtedly raised eyebrows, word of a strange Englischer looking for would cause talk. Amish generally didn't involve themselves in petty gossip, but something of that sort would spread rampant like a wildfire, and her family was suspicious of Englischers. They had seen too many Englischers wanting to have their simple lifestyle, but who could never accept the Ordnung, or devote themselves fully to *Gott*.

Matilda buried her face in her hands. This was the last thing she wanted to deal with while raising her *kinner* alone and grieving.

"Okay, *ja*. I knew him from a long time ago. That's it."

"Why are you so upset?: Lily asked. "He was just asking if I knew you because he happened to be in town for a wedding."

"Wedding?" Matilda lowered her hands. New, unfamiliar emotions churned within her; a small pinch of disappointment and relief mixed together. "He's getting married then?"

"I assume so. I don't know how the Englischers do their weddings. He asked me to help pick out a special wedding gift so I suggested buying a quilt that Almina was selling. You know, the one that is white and has gold stitching?"

"*Ja*."

"He's a rather handsome *Englischer*." Lily remarked, her gaze focused on Matilda. "I still don't know how you know him?"

Matilda started down the sidewalk with Lily catching up to her in a few short strides. She sighed huffily as her sister practically danced her way in front of her and blocked their pathway forcing Matilda to come up short.

"If I tell you how I know him you can't tell anybody, including *maemm* and *Dat*." she said. If you tell anybody I will tell Dat about what I saw today in the fields while you were with Jacob Lapp."

The center of Lily's pale cheeks flushed a bright pink color. She nodded her understanding at the clear warning. "I won't tell anyone. I promise."

Her sister's bright eyes shimmered as she leaned forward, her eagerness clearly apparent. Lily's inquisitive nature always had been a source of problems. With her rumspringa approaching, Matilda genuinely feared for her sister. The temptations from the English life would be too much for her sister's innocent and curious ways. She asked too many questions that often times had troubling answers.

Gott alone knew exactly how much trouble rumspringa had been for Matilda. She offered up a silent, quick prayer and took a deep breath before answering her sister.

"*Ja*, I know Ryan. I met him during rumspringa when I went with Lucy to her *Englischer* Ant's house. We spent most of our time together in the city and when it came time to decide if I wanted to leave, I chose to leave. It wasn't exactly a pleasant goodbye."

Lily took a moment, as if processing what Matilda had said. "He wanted you to stay?"

"*Ja.*" Matilda nodded. "He wanted me to stay behind and give things a chance, but I couldn't stay in the city with all the Englischers anymore."

"I would've stayed behind for him." Lily said with a small smile. The next moment the smile was gone, and she scuffed the bottom of her sneakers on the sidewalk. "I hate it here and all the rules. Sometimes I think being English isn't as bad as everyone claims it to be."

"It's not what you think, Lily. *Ja* some things are better, but it's not worth it to be away from family. How are you going to survive when you're sixteen years old? The English life doesn't work the way it does in our community. It's much harder, and there is far more temptation than what you can handle."

Lily fired back in clear defiance. "I can handle it. Just because you obviously couldn't handle it, doesn't mean I will have the same problem."

"Obviously, I could handle it because I'm standing here. I'm just saying to be cautious, Lily. Rumspringa isn't all you imagine it to be."

"That's your opinion."

Matilda gritted her teeth. When had her little sister, the one who had clung to her hand tightly and pleaded with her to tell another bedtime store, grown up to be so stubborn? She sucked in a calming breath through her nose. "Maybe," she said, "but I am older than you and I was fifteen once too."

"How many years ago was that again?" Lily asked. The fire in her eyes smoldered out into a playful sparkle. They were back on good terms again for the present.

Rolling her eyes in good humor, Matilda twined an arm through Lily's slender one and started their way back down to the Farmer's Market.

"Oh, by the way," Lily started, quilt lacing her words and catching Matilda's attention, "I kinda of told him where you worked. So, expect a visit 'cause he said he would stop by to—"

"You told him where I worked?" Matilda interjected, absolutely horrified at the thought of Ryan showing up to the bakery. "Lily Grace Beachey! You know better than to tell strangers where people work."

"He isn't a stranger, though." Lily said, in full defense mode. "You said that—"

"It doesn't matter if I know him or not. You don't reveal that sort of information to anyone. For all you know that person could have bad intentions."

Lily toed the sidewalk as shame flooded her face. It took all Matilda's restraint to not continue in anger. They were taught not be confrontational towards anyone, but it was hard given the fear budding in Matilda. She prayed *Gott* would help her through this. She loved her sister, loved her dearly, but sometimes her sister's behavior was more than Matilda could handle.

Her thoughts strayed to the morning she realized she was pregnant with Rosella. She had been sitting in the pews alongside Rebecca at church Sunday morning, fighting off the waves of nausea that had plagued her two days after returning home from rumspringa. No longer able to stand it anymore, Matilda had rushed out the barn to empty the contents of her stomach in a field where the cows grazed. It had hit her then, crouching on the ground with achy cramps in her lower back, that her time of the month was supposed to have started five days prior The headaches and soreness of her breast along with the bouts of morning sickness added up to only word: pregnant. She had seen enough women in their community with the same symptoms.

Shame and joy had taken her over, all in a single moment. After all, children were a gift from *Gott*, but the circumstances surrounding Rosella were not what Matilda had prayed and hoped for; not at all. Through the drenching tears, she'd prayed long and hard that *Gott* would give her answer—and soon.

That night, when Samuel took her home in his buggy, Matilda confessed to Samuel. She told him all that had happened during rumspringa, including everything with Ryan. She could still perfectly picture Samuel's eyes as they had flared full with hurt and tears, and how the bright moonlight glinted off them. Despite the jealousy ripping through him, he had remained a gentleman had offered marriage.

She felt so undeserving of his kindness. Matilda knew she wouldn't be shunned because this had all happened during rumspringa before her baptism. Still, the thought of the devastation that would fill her parents when they learned of her activities brought immense pain to Matilda. She didn't want to hurt them or cause them any more pain than necessary. Samuel loved her, and Matilda knew that she shared that love. It seemed the perfect solution to an impossible situation, and she believed *Gott* had granted her some measure of mercy by Samuel's immediate response. *Gott* had a plan and had provided a way. He had answered her prayer: she and Samuel were to share in this precious gift from *Gott*.

After their baptism, they were published by the church a few weeks after that and married at the beginning of November. Her family had been overjoyed when they announced they were having a *bobli*. Despite knowing that he was not the biological father, Samuel had rubbed her belly eagerly and fell in love with Rosella, their precious gift from *Gott*, when she was born. She truly had been a blessing. Not once did they talk about Rosella's biological father after Matilda had told Samuel about her unplanned pregnancy. She would often wonder why Samuel never brought up the subject, but she let it go for her own sanity.

She blinked back the rush of memories. Wetness coated her eyelashes from the tears that had formed, and she reached up to wipe them dry and avoid her sister's obvious concern.

"We should head back. We've been gone longer than we should be," Matilda finally offered.

For once, Lily didn't pry any further.

When they reached the Farmers Market, the crowd of *Englischer's* had dispersed a bit as the afternoon hour approached. Sunlight bore down on them as Matilda split the Snicker's bar into three equal pieces for her *kinner* who ate the candy with pleased smiles. She kept an anxious eye trained on the crowds, searching uneasily for Ryan's trademark honey-blonde hair.

"I think it's time to pack up." Jonathan said. He stood behind the table, staring down at the couple squashes and cucumbers that were left over. "We've sold about everything we can sell with a few vegetables leftover."

Matilda smiled in relief to be done. She wanted nothing more than to retreat to her *haus* and away from the market.

"*Ja*," she said, gathering the remaining vegetables. "I better get the *kinner* home and get some lunch in their bellies.

She handed the vegetables to Isaac and Matthew for them to carry to the buggy. Matilda scanned the crowds for Rosella and spotted the golden strands of her hair glimmering in the sunlight as she danced laughingly around other *kinner* in a game of tag. Her tall and slender frame allowed her to skip away from the shorter *kinner*. Before Matilda could call out, her *maemm* swooped down and picked her discarded prayer *kapp*. She placed it tenderly back on Rosella's head and pressed an affectionate kiss to her forehead.

Matilda cast one last glance around the Farmers Market before climbing into the buggy alongside her *kinner*. As their buggy traveled down the road and crossed an intersection they passed by a black car with heavily tinted windows. The hair on Matilda's arms stood on edge at the sensation of being watched. She peered warily at the car's windshield before continuing down the street.

CHAPTER THREE

C hurch the following morning was at the Byler's barn. Since the mornings were still warm enough to hold church outside, they sat in the barn and took their seats as their minister Larry started to preach.

Matilda kept a watchful eye on her *kinner*. Even though they were well behaved as all Amish *kinner* tended to be, there was the occasional temper tantrum or unruly behavior. Particularly, she kept one eye on Isaac and Matthew as they sat sandwiched between Jonathan and Eli. Neither one had taken too kindly to Eli's presence yet. The scowl permanently etched on Isaac's face was an indicator of his grumpy mood, and she prayed that there wouldn't be an outburst of anger.

She curled her fingers around the copy of the *Ausband* sitting on her lap as they began to sing their usual hymns. It had been Samuel's and sometimes for comfort she would flick through the pages of hymns to read the little notes he had written since his baptism. Once baptized. the *mensleit* took a vow of ministry and one day could be called upon to minister. Samuel took the responsibility seriously, fervently taking notes while their ministers preached and made it a point to be very active with events in their church.

Matilda couldn't have been more proud of him. She still was. The last afternoon before *Gott* took him to heaven, she had caught Samuel struggling out of bed and coughing violently from the movement. He waved away her protests, insisting that it was a nice day out and the fresh mountain air that smelled of pine would clear his lungs. With one arm wrapped around his trim waist, she dutifully helped him down the stairs, along with their *kinner* following behind excitedly. They had taken a blanket and sat on the front lawn to enjoy the late summer together. Samuel took it upon himself that afternoon to protect his "dear flock of sheep" as he would say with a smile and read them scriptures about grief and comfort.

She knew even then that *Gott* had spoken through Samuel and gave her a warning for what was to come. Even when it seemed that Samuel had gotten better during that hour of laughing in the summer breeze, the community doctor had said his lungs were filled with fluid and his fevers were high. It would only be a matter of time before he could no longer breathe, and they did everything they could in that short amount of time, but she had still felt helpless while watching Samuel struggle to draw in each and every breath.

A teardrop splattered on the page. She wiped her eyes dry and glanced to the right, praying that her *maemm* hadn't seen it. Rebecca naturally did, and tuned to her *kinner's* emotional and spiritual needs just as Matilda was with her own *kinner*. Rebecca arched an eyebrow in concern and rested a soft hand on Matilda's knee.

What was wrong with me?

Matilda bit her bottom lip. Even in grief she had always managed to keep control over her emotions for the sake of her *kinner* who looked to her constantly for guidance since

Samuel's death. The black color of her *kapp* and dress was enough to indicate her mourning, but Matilda had always somewhat prided herself on keeping control of her emotions even when it threatened to rip her apart. She saved it for the privacy of her bedroom and well into the night hours.

Chewing on her bottom lip in contemplation, Matilda stared out the window. Yesterday had been nothing but terrifying. Her daughter had come across her real father and hadn't even realized it. While Matilda knew her secret had died with Samuel nine months ago, with Ryan's appearance yesterday she felt that secret threatening to rise up from the grave absent Samuel, and it terrified her beyond anything. If Rosella found out or her community... Matilda shook those thoughts away. She couldn't even think about the possible ramifications.

Yet she couldn't stop the questions. Why was Ryan here after so many years? Was there some sort of reason behind *Gott* bringing him back into her life?

None of it seemed fair or even logical. The terrified part of her prayed for *Gott* to keep Ryan away. Only a small part of her felt tempted to see Ryan after so many years. Except it wouldn't be temptation, she reminded herself. He was getting married and most likely wouldn't show up to the bakery. She took some sort of comfort in that.

Hymns concluded shortly before lunch time. Matilda helped the other women spread out the various breads, pastries, cheeses, and salads across a large table specifically built to hold lunch for Fellowship on Sundays. She had just placed her breakfast casserole that consisted of hash browns, scrambled eggs, bacon, and melted cheddar cheese when Isaac appeared at her side.

"Mama," he said, tugging on the skirts of her dress to gain her attention, "I want to go home."

Matilda smoothed down an errant strand of jet black hair that stuck up in same spot Samuel's hair did and smiled down at her son. "We will go home after we have Fellowship. Let me make you a—"

"I want to go home, now!"

Isaac stomped a foot as frustration filled his pale face. Sensing a temper tantrum about to spark, Matilda pulled Isaac away from the church members who were watching sympathetically. She bent down so that she and Isaac were at eye level and spoke quietly, "Listen to me, Isaac. We are not going home until Fellowship is over."

He crossed his arms and pushed out his bottom lip. "I want to go home, Mama. I'm tired and not hungry."

"Well, I'm sorry, but we aren't leaving because you feel tired." Matilda answered. "Now if you—"

"It's not fair!" he said, the words spurting forth while his eyes blazed in a display of temper. "Why can't we do what *I* want sometimes?"

Matilda sighed, her exasperation increasing by the minute. She had no idea where Isaac's tantrums came from since they had developed over the past few months, but had a growing suspicion that it came from missing his *daed* and not understanding why Samuel had died. She couldn't understand it herself sometimes, and only imagined how frustrating it was to her *kinner*. It broke her heart. Before she could say anything she felt a hand rest on her shoulder.

"Don't talk back to your *maemm*, Isaac." Eli's voice cut in. "You'll leave whenever Fellowship is over. I don't want to hear you throwing a tantrum again."

Isaac's gaze revealed his sudden anger as he stared Eli's hand resting on Matilda's shoulder. She eased her way out from beneath his touch and moved way, in some part to control her own uneasy temper.

"You can't tell me what to do! You're not my *daed*," Isaac yelled, before fleeing the room.

Matilda buried her face in her hands in exhaustion. Then she resolutely straightened her prayer *kapp* as it had been knocked loose when Isaac ran away.

"Don't worry." Eli said, resting his hands once again on her shoulders.. "*Kinner* don't understand how to grieve. He'll be fine in time."

Blessed are those who mourn, for they will be comforted.

That had been the last scripture Samuel ever read from the book of Matthew, his favorite. Except she had been anything but comforted at that moment.

Matilda faced Eli, and his hands fell away. "I appreciate your help," she said, attempting to control her voice but hearing its flatness "but I think I know my *kinner* better than you."

Visibly shaken at her response, Eli attempted an answer. "I'm sorry.. I was just trying to help. I didn't think mean anything."

She felt a creeping shame come over her for her unbecoming behavior, and in such a public way. Matilda sighed and massaged her temples. Finally, she offered a contrite smile. "I am the one who is sorry. I don't know what has gotten into me."

"No one's judging you." Eli replied, raising a hand toward her shoulder in a cmoforting gesture only to stop in mid-air. "We're all here to help in any way we can."

Matilda nodded her head, squeezing his fingers before taking a step back. They walked side by side towards their community gathered around the tables of food. Her heart warmed in the presence of her all these people who offered a helping hand, and opened their hearts in kindness.

Maybe things wouldn't be so bad.

The aroma of freshly sliced peaches with sugar filled Matilda's nose in the most pleasant way when she stepped into her *maemm's* bakery. She heard her sneakers squeak on the clean linoleum floor, announcing her presence, as she walked behind the counter and into the kitchen.

"*Gut* morning!" Rebecca greeted. She stood alongside Lily, demonstrating how to crimp a pie crust. "You're just in time. I need you to help your sister make pies since the last two she baked burned."

Indeed, two pies that looked like charred remains sat on the counter near the kitchen door. The apple of Lily's fair cheeks turned a beet root shade of red as she looked down to hide her embarrassment. Matilda's heart softened for her young sister, still learning how to bake and prepare herself for married life.

Matilda shrugged out of her black woolen coat and placed it by the back door. She pushed away the tumultuous thoughts of Ryan being in town that had plagued her all morning.

"Of course, Mama. We will have all the pies baked in no time." With that she gave her sister a smile hoping to offer some comfort.

The second Rebecca disappeared to the front of the store tears filled Lily's eyes. Burying her head in her hands, she leaned forward toward the counte. Her muffled cries echoed throughout the kitchen. Matilda wrapped her sister in her arms and tried to help control the trembling. Then pulled back and stared at that lovely but tear-stained face she so loved.

"Come now, no tears. All of us have burned pies at some point." She said, gently tucking a strand of hair behind Lily's ear. With a gentle, soothing touch, she rubbed Lily's bacl as an elderly woman's voice filled the bakery. They had their customer of the day. She offered a towel to Lily to dry her face. "We all learn in time. That's why Mama has you working here."

"*Ja,*." Lily's voice remained thick with emotion as she patted her tear-stained cheeks. "But you and Mama are the bakers of the family. What am I going to offer to my future *mann*?"

"You're only fifteen years old, Lily. Rumspringa hasn't even started yet for you. There's still time for you to learn baking and cooking. Tell you what," Matilda said as she cupped her sister's jaw tenderly in the palm of her hand. Using the pads of her thumbs, she wiped away a few tears s trailing down her sister's face, "Come over to my *haus* on the Sundays we don't have church and I'll teach you myself how to cook."

Lily brightened at Matilda's offer. "Really?" she asked, and finally allowed a genuine smile to slip past the remaining tears. "You would do that for me?"

"Of course. You're my sister, and I want to help." Before she say more, Lily threw her arms around Matilda and squeezed her tightly.

"Danka!"

The two sisters resumed work with Matilda showing her how to pinch the pie crusts for the perfect crimp and how to accurately measure out sugar by using a knife to skim excess sugar off the measuring cup. Tutoring her sister offered a needed distraction from the growing sense of anxiety burning a hole in the center of her chest. While she kept a smile on her face, Matilda made sure she kept one ear strained for the sound of the front door opening. When the morning passed by without a glimpse of Ryan anywhere, she allowed herself to relax. Surely, if he planned to stop by he would have done so by now.

By the time Rebecca returned to the kitchen, peach pies and apple pies, all with latticed tops, lined the counters.

"Lily..." Rebecca breathed out, gazing at the pies in evident shock. "You make all these yourself?"

"*Ja*, Mama," Lily said, and then nodded toward Matilda. who was busy pulling out a bubbling rhubarb pie. "Of course, with Matilda's help. She's going to give me baking lessons every Sunday we don't have church."

"That's *gut*. I'm very proud of you."

Lily beamed, clearly happily, at their *maemm* and continued to crimp another pie crust the way Matilda had showed her.

"Ach, Matilda." Rebecca came to a stand alongside her oldest daughter and handed over a piece of paper. "There is a wedding tomorrow, and here are the requested pies that need to be baked before lunch time."

Matilda stared down at her *maemm's* elegant handwriting: Snitz Pie, Whoopie pie, Shoofly Pie, Lemon Custard Pie. The variety surprised her but she nodded. "I'll start baking them right now."

"*Gut.* The snitz is in that bowl for you. I got this order late afternoon yesterday so I was able to let the snitz soak overnight."

"Can I help?" Lily asked, rushing to Matilda's sode. "I want to learn how to make Snitz pie."

Matilda paused before she answered. Snitz pie required a bit more experience to bake. The dried apples were soaked overnight in water and then cooked over low heat until the slices were soft and easily mash-able. With the pies going to the wedding tomorrow, she would have to tend to them carefully and she doubted that Lily's baking skills could handle them. She smiled gently at her sister's eager face, but it was Rebecca who spoke first.

"*Nee*, Lily. These pies require more baking skills that you don't have just yet. Let your sister handle them and you continue to do the other pies."

Once again, water filled Lily's eyes, no doubt at their *maemm's* curtness. Lily said nothing, thought, and returned to her work area to finish scooping out peach filling. Matilda gave an inward sigh at their *maemm's* behavior. As caring and loving as Rebecca could be, she had a sharp tongue when it came to certain things she believed to be easy. Sometimes Matilda felt the urge to remind her *maemm* that she had years and years of experience in baking and being a *fraa*, so unlike Lily who had no real experience yet.

Matilda lost herself in the motions of baking the ordered pies, and the familiar work served as an efficient distraction from her strained nerves. When she finished the pies, there was a half hour to spare before noon, so she decided to take a quick break before Rebecca's lunch break and stepped outside.

The Sangre de Cristo Mountains and the San Juan Mountains were covered in their usually fiery reds and bright yellows, even more vibrant than last weekend with the rapid temperature drop. Matilda gazed out at them, leaning back against the wall, and gave herself up to the wave of serenity that crashed over her. She loved the fall, and it had always been Samuel's favorite season as well. They would both spend hours sitting on their front porch taking in splendor and sharing whatever would come to mind.

How she missed those moments.

Her exchange with Eli yesterday during Fellowship remained with her and a heavy guilt hung over her as she remembered her response. She owed him an apology. She stared out across the land toward the horizon. On the way home, she would make sure to stop by his haus with a Whoopie pie.

Feeling much more at ease, Matilda stepped back into the kitchen right as the little bell on the bakery's front door jingled as the door opened. She gave the clock on the wall a quick glance and hurried to the freshly baked pies. Her *maemm's* cheerful voiced echoed in the bakery as she greeted the customer, "Hello there, sir. What can I help you with?"

"I'm here to pick up some pies for Amber Myers. She said she called in yesterday afternoon about having them baked for a wedding."

A trickle of familiarity with the voice caused Matilda to pause while in the midst of wrapping the pies in cellophane. She'd heard that voice before.

"Oh yes," Rebecca said, "my daughter baked them and they are ready. Please, let me know if you need anything else. I will be taking my lunch now so let me fetch her and the pies."

Her *maemm* appeared in the doorway then and motioned for her to hurry. Wrapping the last of the pies with cellophane, Matilda brushed by Rebecca cradling the pies in her arms. She placed them on the counter. When she raised her head, she met the gaze of two perfect sapphire pools who peered at her curiously.

Matilda lost all function. Her world rolled to a stop; her heart faltered. The Englischer standing before her was the same one from the Farmers Market. Honey-blonde wisps of hair danced airily across his strong forehead and his brow furrowed as he gazed at her. Her own traitorous eyes drank steadily of the fair-headed and handsome man who stood before her, from his broad shoulders and chest straining against the white tee-shirt he wore to the cleanly shaven jaw.

"Ryan," His name carried out on the release of her breath.

His frown deepened even more. "I'm sorry. Do I know you?"

He didn't recognize her. The knowledge cut her. He wouldn't, of course, she thought, allowing reason to staunch the pain. The last time they had seen each other was at the coffee shop in the bookstore called Barns & Nobles, and she was newly seventeen then dressed in English clothes. He had never seen her in traditional Amish clothes or in her prayer *kapp*.

She cleared her throat and managed to keep her voice steady. "I don't think so. That is the name of the person I was told who would pick up the pies."

She hated hearing how the lie spilled so easily from her lips and hurriedly rang up the pies before he recognized her. Maitlda had no desire to confront old feelings for Ryan at all, let alone while mourning for her *mann*, or risk having the community hear the truth about Rosella's birth.

Before Ryan could reply, Lily walked through the doorframe and came to Matilda's side. "Matilda, the pies are—"

Ryan's eyes widened. He reared back and stared at Matilda.

"—beginning to burn on the edges. What do I do?"

A long pause followed.

Matilda kept her eyes focused everywhere other than on Ryan standing in front of her. Lily glanced back and forth between them in apparent confusion before the recognition began and that familiar mischievous smile appeared. "You're the Englischer named Ryan from the Farmers Market."

His met her gaze. "Yes, you helped me pick out a wedding gift. What was your name again?"

"Lily." She held out a hand for Ryan to shake. "See, Matilda. He's not so bad like you—"

"Line the pie edges with tinfoil so they don't burn anymore," Matilda cut in, staring long enough for her sister to get the message.

Lily shared her disappointment with Matilda by giving her a big scowl. Clearly she didn't like being shooed from the room, but she did as she was told. Matilda and Ryan stood face to face in awkward silence. Matilda twisted her hands nervously in front of her and kept her eyes downcast as she felt Ryan;s intense study. It was one of the most nerve-wracking experiences in all her life.

"Wow, Mattie..." Ryan started, his voice faltering slightly, "You look good. It's been a long time."

The sound of his voice, deep and syrupy, wove through her surreally. That voice always had a strong affect on her, stronger than a sip of alcohol that would flip her world upside down. Just like that she. was sixteen again and feeling her heart skip a beat as she felt him focus only on her. She inhaled sharply, willing her heart to stop the hard pounding so she could and regain control over herself.

"*Jah*. It's been a long time," Matilda replied.

Ryan rubbed the back of his neck and shifted on the balls of his feet. He looked torn between feeling uncomfortable and happy to see her. Matilda took a deep breath and prayed to *Gott* for the strength to keep her composure.

"I've been looking for you," he said, his voice suddenly quiet.

The statement made Matilda smile wryly despite the warning bells ringing in her head. "I've heard. My sister told me that you even looked for me in Lancaster."

"I did." He nodded, a grimace flashing on his face. "By the way, you left out the fact that the Amish have a tendency to be a little protective over each other. All they would tell me is that you moved to Colorado."

"It's not every day a strange Englischer asks about someone in the community." she replied, ready to end the conversation. Any minute her *maemm* would return from her lunch break. Seeing Ryan still in the bakery would arouse her curiosity. Matilda looked pointedly down at the credit card in Ryan's hand. "The total is $23.00. Just pop these into the oven for a few minutes to warm them up and—"

"I was looking for you because I wanted to thank you."

"Thank me?" She echoed, confused. "What do you have to thank me for?"

"You know—" Ryan said, handing over the credit card. Their fingers brushed and a sizzling sensation shot up Matilda's arm at the brief contact. "For helping me realize that there truly is a God watching over this crazy world."

Matilda was speechless. The last thing she ever expected to come from Ryan Meyers was an admission to believing in God. She remembered how he had scoffed at God and anyone living his life to worship Him. It had been one of the reasons why Matilda knew she couldn't be in a relationship with him. Even at seventeen, her faith had been ingrained deeply within her. Living any other way didn't seem right.

Then again, she thought, so many things could happen since she last saw him. After all, she'd been married and widowed in the same time. So yes, anything was possible with *Gott's* will.

"*Gott* found you, Ryan. He was always looking for you. I had nothing to do with it."

Matilda slid the plastic card through the credit card reader and tore off the receipt for Ryan to sign. His wrist moved fluidly before handing both items back and this time she was careful to not touch his fingers.

"Not *Gott*, as you call Him. It was pretty much you that inspired me to go back to Him." Ryan said, sliding the card back into his wallet. He smiled wryly as she sent him a dubious. "I've been thinking about you a lot lately this past year. There are things in my life that aren't—" he paused to sigh heavily, "—well they aren't good and it got me thinking of everything that you had said to me so many years ago when you were on your runchspringa. What?"

"Rumspringa," Matilda corrected, laughing. "It's called rumspringa."

Ryan waved a dismissive hand. "Same thing. Forgive me, the Pennsylvania Dutch you taught me is a little bit rusty. I wanted to say I'm sorry, too, for how I reacted the last time we saw each other and about you leaving. It wasn't right at all."

She hadn't even given their rather tense goodbye a second thought after returning home. There had been several other things that happened afterwards she worried about more, and a gut instinct told her that Ryan didn't spend his time searching for her just to apologize.

Before a tempting thought could form, Matilda took a step back from the register and reminded herself that Ryan was getting married.

"You should know that the Amish don't hold grudges, so you were forgiven a long time ago."

He gave her that charming smile that so lit up his face, and she couldn't help but notice how the light in his sapphire eyes that looked so eerily like Rosella's danced happily. Just like that Matilda, was seventeen years old again with wobbly knees and butterflies fluttering violently in her stomach.

"That's good to hear." Ryan said, then leaned forward and placed his hands squarely on the counter. "I really hope you're happy with whomever you married."

Her heart clenched painfully, but she forced herself to nod politely in thanks. He didn't realize the meaning of her wearing black and she didn't have the strength to tell him why. "Thank you, I hope you're happy with your upcoming marriage as well."

"Marriage?" He said and frowned, his fingers drumming the counter. "Who said I was getting married?"

"My *maemm*. She said the pies were for a wedding."

"Right. They are. They're for my sister's wedding though. I'm not the one getting married."

CHAPTER FOUR

Y ou're not getting married?"

Matilda's heart palpitated. He wasn't getting married? She felt her lower stomach tighten with dread, and she hastily looked down at the stack of pies between them to avoid Ryan's curious stare.

"No," Ryan repeated. "Who told you that I was getting married?"

"I thought my younger sister was helping you pick out a wedding gift for your wedding."

Matilda knew she shouldn't but she risked a glance upwards to gauge his reaction and saw him flatten his hand over his tousled hair. "Yeah, I said I was picking out a gift for a wedding. The bride and groom don't buy gifts for each other, Mattie."

The offhand comment, innocent as it was, played on Matilda's already strained mood. A few times she had wondered what happened to Ryan, where he was in the world, but seeing him for the first time since Rumspringa and months after Samuel's death only heightened her confusion.

A headache made its presence known at the back of her head and pounded forward forward. Before she could excuse herself, in desperate need of some quiet time, the front door of the bakery opened and a slender woman with mirroring honey blonde hair walked in. A cloud of perfume that smelled dimly of rose petals filled the bakery as the woman approached the counter with her heels clacking against the linoleum floor. The startling resemblance between the two of them from their matching hair color and eyes told her who it was before any introductions. Matilda wracked her brain, sorting through her memories with Ryan to try to recall his sister's name.

"What's going on?" she questioned, her cool gaze flicking between the two of them. A frown marred her smooth face that had layers of makeup. "I've been waiting in the car for ten minutes. We have to get over to the floral shop and pick up all the flowers to hand over to the wedding planner since—"

"Olivia," Ryan said, smoothly cutting through his sister's monologue. "I was in the middle of a conversation when you so rudely interrupted. Mattie, this is my sister Olivia. She is the one getting married tomorrow."

Matilda gave the woman her best smile even though she made no attempt to hide her immediate assessment of Matilda.

Olivia tapped the counter with her rather lengthy manicured nails and finally addressed Matilda. "Pleasure, Mattie." Olivia said, her voice crisp on the edges. "I apologize for being so rude. I did not realize that my brother was in the middle of a conversation with an Amish woman or, as some of you call yourselves, Plain."

Matilda felt the flame surge to her face. There was no mistaking the insult and it took all Matilda's strength to temper her response. Amish were not confrontational, even when challenged.

She saw Ryan's face, the lines tighening around his eyes and the withering look he sent in Olivia's direction. His sister missed it entirely as a display of jams caught her attention and she and her heels clacked away from them.

"I'm sorry about Olivia," he said once Olivia was out of ear shot. "She's not like that usually. She's turned into a bridezella since the maid of honor bailed on her, the original baker screwed up the wedding cake order, and the florist called in sick with the flu. It's been one hell of a weekend."

Matilda merely felt baffled over the meaning of "bridezilla" and the plans he described. Amish weddings were simple ceremonies as much as they were beautiful. They relied on family to harvest the celery crops, bake the dishes, and prepare the haus for the community. An English wedding sounded much more complicated. It was no wonder that Olivia had become this "bridezella" thing.

"Mattie?"

The sound of her name pulled her away from her thoughts of stressful English weddings. When she she looked, Ryan had a strange expression. She remembered how those sapphire depths could peer right into her soul and divine whatever was going on with her.

Ryan leaned forward over the counter and a cloud of his fresh cologne enveloped them.. She closed her, remember the smell. It was the same as when she first met him. Lucy had suggested going to a night club, but the music, and provocative dancing had been too much for Matilda. Instead, she found herself walking to the library with Ryan giving her his sweater when she shivered, and inhaling the fresh cologne made her dizzy.

"I really am happy to see you again. Is there any way we could catch up?" Ryan asked. " I understand if your husband wouldn't like the idea, but I really would like to tell you everything that has happened."

"I—"

They were interrupted when the bakery door opened again. This time Rebecca stepped through, her lunch pail dangling from her hand. She raised that eyebrow of hers at the sight of Ryan and leaning over the counte, no doubt. Matilda felt the heat from her m*aemm's* stare and took a swift step backwards, effectively putting distance between herself and Ryan. Her *maemm* almost strolled toward the counter. Her pursed lips stretched into a small smile as she took in Ryan's appearance.

"Can we help you?" Rebecca inquired, coming to Matilda's side in a protective gesture. The sideways glance gave Matilda the permission she needed to back away from the register and the opportunity to flee.

"I was just picking up the pies for the wedding." Ryan said and edged backwards himself after he gathered up the pies. "Nice seeing you again, Mattie. I'm sure that I'll see you around since I'm in town for a while."

Olivia immediately flanked Ryan's side as they walked out of the bakery loaded with pies. Once the door slammed shut behind them, a magnetic silence filled the front end of the bakery. Matilda's skin still prickled from the promise lacing Ryan's voice, but she also felt Rebecca's heated stare. She didn't have to wait long for the the expected outburst.

"How do you know that Englischer? Is this the same one that Lily told me about? The one looking for you?" Rebecca demanded, propping her hands on her hips.

"I don't know him."

Matilda comforted herself in the knowledge that there was some truth in that. She didn't know know him anymore, and, she barely knew him years ago. Their time together had been short, so short even for all that had happened. People change over time.

"Ma, I need to go home—"

"He obviously knows who you are, Matilda. I don't know how you know him, but you best keep your distance."

Matilda concentrated on her breathing. It wasn't like her *maemm* to tell her what to do. Parents typically never involved themselves in their *kinner's* lives when it came to courtship or marriage, but Rebecca had always done so to a degree. She had been more than ecstatic about Matilda marrying Samuel and now that he was gone she seemed determined to push Matilda towards Eli. Several times Matilda had to remind herself that Rebecca was a *maemm*, no matter the age of her *kinner*. Matilda knew from raising her own *kinner* that she shared the same concern and worry about her *kinner* and knew age wouldn't matter.

She pinched the bridge of her nose in distress and caught sight of a piece of paper fluttering around on the counter. It was the receipt for the order of pies Ryan left behind. Her gaze lifted in time to see Ryan's frame passing by the front window, so she retreated to the kitchen before the conversation could go any further

"I'll check on Lily and start baking those cookies." she said, without sparring Rebecca a second glance.

The bell jingled right as Matilda slipped through the door of the kitchen. She let out a pent-up breath and leaned back against the wall in relief to be out of her *maemm* and Ryan's sight. Across the kitchen, Lily paused in wrapping a pie in cellophane and opened her mouth, but quickly shut it at Matilda's warning look.

Her heart still pounded furiously in the caverns of her chest and made it hard to hear the conversation that happened next.

"I'm sorry. I forgot my rec—"

"Quite all right. Here it is. Have a good day."

A tense pause followed. Matilda waited for the bell above the door to jingle or footsteps, but it was Rebecca's strained voice that broke the silence, "Is there something else I can do for you?"

The question came out as a challenge despite the friendly tone in Rebecca's voice. She heard Ryan clear his throat awkwardly, apparently unsure of what to do. Matilda's eyes closed as she quietly began to pray that Ryan would let it be and not say anything about how they knew each other.

"No, ma'am. I was just wondering if I could put in another request for a pie? My sister and I have heard great things about your bakery from the local community and we want a few ourselves."

Matilda couldn't believe what she was hearing. They needed more pies? A shuffle of pens clinking in the glass jar and paper being ripped from a pad echoed in the bakery.

"What type of pie would you like us to bake?" Rebecca asked, not bothering to thank him for the compliment; a tell-tale sign that she was still suspicious of his presence as it was common courtesy to thank someone when they complimented her bakery.

"I'd love a Whoopie pie. Someone told me that Mattie makes those and they—"

There it was. The subtle slip of Matilda's nickname that no one in her family ever used. It was only Ryan who said it, and she could practically hear Rebecca's teeth grinding in her attempt to remain calm.

"I don't know how you know my daughter or what your intentions are exactly—"

"My intentions?" Ryan echoed, clearly amused by whatever Rebecca was implying. "I'm sorry, but you don't know who I am, and—"

"It doesn't matter who you are. My daughter has enough to worry about with raising her *kinner* on her own and taking care of her *haus* and farm. I appreciate your business, but I think it's best if you left us alone."

"Of course. I didn't mean to offend anyone, but I'd still like to order a Whoopie pie for tomorrow."

Footsteps scuffled out of the bakery. Matilda thumped her head back against the wall, and exhaustion crashed down on her. Why was this happening now? Everything was already hard enough, but now Ryan had complicated it even more without realizing it.

"What's going on?" Lily asked. She dusted her hands clean from flour, wiping them on her white apron and took in Matilda's sagged form in bafflement. "Why are—wait, where are you going?"

Matilda suddenly straightened and went to the pegs next to the back door. She snatched her coat, slipping her arms hurriedly through the sleeves. It was childish to be running away from her *maemm*, but she needed the time to pray and reflect before picking her *kinner* up from school.

"Tell Ma that I'm feeling a bit sick and that I'll be back tomorrow morning for work" she tossed out over her shoulder, before slipping out into the slightly chilled afternoon. Careful to avoid the other side of the building, Matilda went to the field where they kept their buggy and horses during the day. Pepper (Rosella's name for their horse) lifted her head from where she was grazing at Matilda's approaching steps, her ears twitching in excitement.

"Sorry, Pepper. I forgot to grab your carrots." Matilda said, scratching Pepper's chin affectionately. She laughed when Pepper snorted her discontentment at that, but followed Matilda out of the field to be hitched up.

The leather reigns felt cold and solid in Matilda's fingers as she directed Pepper in their direction of their *haus*. Her eyes slipped closed in relief to be out in the refreshing air tinged with winter's coolness as tried to push Ryan's sudden appearance from her mind.

Except he wasn't easily pushed out.

"Matilda?"

Eli tugged his leather gloves off and peered down at the ground from where he currently stood on top of his roof. Shingles were scattered in the lawn from when he had ripped them free to replace with new ones. Matilda cupped a hand over eyes so she could gaze upwards, offering him a small smile.

"What are you doing up there?" she asked.

"There was a soft spot on the roof I've had my eye on for a while. I wanted to make sure it was patched before the first snowfall."

Eli walked lithely along the side of the roof and to the ladder propped up on the far side of the *haus*. She held her breath nervously and followed him from the ground, keeping a cautious eye on his feet in case he slipped.

"What are you doing here? Is everything okay?"

She had no idea why she decided to turn down the road to Eli's *haus*. It was either Pepper or herself that stirred them in Eli's direction, but either way her heart warmed at the sight of him. The ladder trembled as Eli quickly descended it and jumped down from the third step, landing surely on his feet facing Matilda. His straw hat fell from the top of his head and revealed the short strands of his auburn hair.

"*Ja.* Everything is fine..." Matilda trailed off as a wave of emotions took over. Tears moistened her eyes and the whole time Eli watched her slowly crumple inwards, his head tilted to the side in concern. "I just—I just wanted to apologize for my behavior at church yesterday when all you were trying to do was help. That's all you've ever done is try to help."

Eli blinked at the apology and wrinkles appeared along his forehead when he frowned at her, shaking his head. "I don't understand why you are apologizing, Matilda. You know that we don't hold grudges and that I forgave you the second you walked away. What's going on?"

For the longest time Samuel and she carried the secret of Rosella's conception. When Samuel died the entire weight of it fell onto Matilda's shoulders and with the past hour's events playing repeatedly in her mind, the weight was too heavy. Her already weakened shoulders would surely fail in her effort to keep it.

She discreetly studied Eli from beneath her wet lashes. He was so much like Samuel with his compassion and strength, but there were stark differences as well. Could she tell him? It wasn't in the Amish way to judge or to turn away someone in spiritual need, but she didn't want to burden Eli with her problems and confusion. He had lost his *fraa* and was left raising his *kinner* alone while trying to help Matilda with the upkeep of her own farm and *haus*.

It was fear that kept Matilda's mouth shut. A part of her didn't want to admit that she had grown close to Eli over the past nine months and relied on his comforting presence through the hard days, but she would be lost without him. She would be lost without her community and their willingness to lend a hand.

"It was just a hard day at the bakery is all," Matilda said, wiping her face dry of tears. She bent down and picked up Eli's straw hat, handing it to him. "I didn't mean to intrude on your one day off from your job."

One day out of the week Eli took time off to do things around the *haus* and spend time with his *kinner*. Other days he was either out of town doing construction jobs or trying to keep up with his farm. He never complained once because hard work was the solid foundation in their way of life.

"You never intrude, Matilda. I owe you an apology as well," Eli said, placing his hat back on. "I didn't mean to make things more difficult for you the other day with Isaac. I know how hard it is to parent alone and how your *kinner* feel about losing Samuel."

Matilda's heart clenched thinking of how hard her *kinner* had struggled over the months. Rosella had taken it the hardest being older and understanding what death meant. Isaac and Matthew, however, would ask repeatedly where their *daed* was and would promptly burst into tears when Matilda told them he was in Heaven and that they couldn't visit until the right time. It took everything in her to not cry while watching the tears fill their eyes and the devastation that followed.

The same emotions swirling within her glimmered in Eli's eyes. Out of impulse, she reached out to grab his rough hand in her softer one and their fingers laced together. She found herself reciting the passage Samuel had circled, "Blessed are those who mourn, for they will be comforted."

A small smile curled up Eli's lips. They were silent for a while, taking in each other's presence as comfort, and listening to the rustling of the leaves trickling down from tree branches. For that moment at least a sense of peace came to her as she stood by Eli's side taking in autumn's colors as it always did whenever she took in *Gott's* creation.

The pressure of Eli's fingers squeezing hers brought Matilda's attention to their joined hands between them. In time, she could get used to feeling of Eli's fingers between her own instead of Samuel's. They felt reassuringly warm and real like she was no longer holding a ghost of Samuel's hand.

Her thoughts returned to the bakery earlier. Ryan wasn't a part of her world and would never be. She could never picture him adapting to the Amish church or accepting the *Ordnung*. There was no explanation to his sudden appearance in her life; quite frankly, she was too afraid to figure out why. She couldn't let the emotional temptation take over her and let her imagination run wild like it had done during rumspringa. She had to be strong for her *kinner's* sake. If she could be strong for them, then she could be strong herself later.

CHAPTER FIVE

The smell of melted butter and apples filled the bakery. Matilda scooped the apple mixture out of the bowl and placed it into the crimped pie crust, spreading it evenly with the back of a spoon. Her fingers trembled when she picked up the strips of sliced pie crust, latticing them across the top and then she placed the in the hot oven to bake. In an hour Ryan would return to pick up his pie, and the very thought twisted her stomach into knots.

Matilda glanced over her shoulder at Lily kneading bread dough and lost in her own thoughts. With nothing in the oven besides Ryan's pie, she left her sister and picked up a dusting rag. If she had to wait for Ryan to come back then the least she could do was clean the bakery.

While she dusted down shelves and organized loaves of breads, her thoughts strayed back to the dream she had the night before.

She stood on the front porch. A snowfall trickled down from the grey clouds. She shielded her eyes against the whiteness covering the land, and stared across the field to where her children were throwing snowballs at one another in obvious delight. Her heart softened with a tender and burning love

Strong arms snaked around her waist, startling her from her observations and the smell of *kaffee* filled her nose. She leaned back against the strong form pressed up against her back and giggled when a beard nuzzled the side of her neck fondly.

"You should be upstairs resting," she said.

Familiar hands found her gloved ones, and she could feel the coldness of the afternoon through the scratchy wool. Matilda tilted her head to the side, giving her better access to look at Samuel closely. A layer of sweat still clung to his pale skin from the fever that broke only an hour ago, and the strands of his black hair were plastered to his forehead. Dark eyes twinkled playfully with their usual warmth as Samuel's arms tightened around her more.

"I couldn't miss the first snowfall of the winter season," he said.

A snowball flew by them and splattered against the front door. Their *kinner* gazed over at them innocently, hands loose by their sides and matching grins. Samuel's arms lowered from Matilda's waist, and ignoring her protests, he stepped out into the snowy air in their direction.

Matilda followed behind him. "Samuel King! Get back inside. You are not well enough for this—oof!"

Cold snow blinded her for a moment as she sputtered unattractively. She opened her eyes to glare at Samuel grinning innocently at her, snow dripping down from his pink fingers.

"I swear, you are no older than your children sometimes," she huffed at him.

"Perhaps," Samuel replied easily, scooping up another ball of snow. "Let's say you and I teach our *kinner* how to have a proper snowball fight."

Their *kinner* screamed in delight at the challenge, tossing snowballs in Samuel's direction. She bent down to scoop up snow in her hands and formed a ball, aiming it directly at Matthew.

"I think they are in need of a good lesson."

Fluffy snowflakes dampened the top of Matilda's prayer *kapp*. Between the snowfall and snowballs flying around in the air she lost sight of her family. She kept scooping up snowballs, laughing so hard that her lungs hurt, and felt arms go about her waist again.

"Not again, Samuel!" Matilda squirmed in a good attempt, but the arms would not let up. She turned around to mock glare at him, but sapphire eyes greeted her instead of the expected chocolate ones. Her heart froze, and the rest of her body followed suit as she quickly realized in horror who was holding her.

"Let me go, Ryan."

His arms refused to budge, and he stared up at her with an indescribable glint. The snow continued to fall around them, and her traitorous mind focused on the warmth that seemed to radiate off him. Matilda fought with all her strength to be let go, but the harder she struggled the tighter his hold.

"Mama, who is that?" Rosella's voice sliced through the snowy afternoon. Her sapphire eyes flicked to Ryan and then back to where Samuel stood by motionlessly with a snowball still clutched in his hand. "Who is that man, Papa? Why does he look so familiar?"

Matilda's throat thickened. The bottom of her stomach fell to the bottom of her feet, and blood roared within her veins. She continued to struggle against the vice-like grip around her waist and reached for Samuel as snow surrounded him in a tornado of white.

"Samuel, please. Help me!"

He blinked once only in response, a sad smile spreading across his face. "*Nee*, Matilda. This is whom you've always wanted."

Matilda's stomach churned thinking of the dream. She blinked back against the tears clouding her eyes and continued to wipe down the shelves. The dream had been so vivid and real, bordering on a memory. The few widows in their community assured her that the dreams were a part of the grieving process as were the couple of times that Matilda found herself talking to Samuel as though he was sitting in the living room across from her while she sewed. It was funny how much she had built herself around Samuel and didn't realize it until after he was gone.

The jingle of the bell broke her thoughts and brought her thoroughly to the present. She sucked in a breath, unconsciously shrinking back to the wall. This was it. *Gott* would protect her from unsafe temptations or emotions. His strength lived in her strongly.

Boots thumped along the white linoleum floor. Matilda squeezed a loaf of bread to her chest, smashing the soft slices, and held her breath as the boots approached.

"Matilda?"

She deflated when she heard Eli's deep honeyed voice in the bakery. She had regrouped all her strength for nothing. She walked down the aisle of bread and peered around the corner in slight irritation.

"*Ja?* What is it, Eli?"

Eli turned in the direction of her voice. He fidgeted with the brim of his straw hat, something he did more in Matilda's presence.

"I know you're busy here, but I-I-I need your help with something."

A red hue filled the center of his cheeks. Matilda looked at him questioningly, but gestured for him to continue.

"My oldest, Betty, just turned twelve as you know and-well—" He stuttered off, blushing even brighter now.

Matilda stared at Eli in bewilderment. For as long as she had known him, Eli always somehow maintained his composure. Then she realized what he meant with the rather uncomfortable and pointed glance he gave her.

"Ach, I see. Does she require some help?" she asked kindly.

"*Ja*, much of it. She's very, um, emotional and—"

"You have no idea what to do?" Matilda offered, smiling at the visible relief on his face.

"That's exactly it. I have no idea what to do. She's in the buggy right now, and the teacher sent her home for the day to deal with...things."

The irritation and nerves from her dream floated away, at least temporarily. She only imagined what it was like to be a widowed father and trying to raise two girls reaching puberty. Her motherly instincts kicked in.

Matilda set the smashed loaf of bread on the counter and poked her head in the door to tell Lily she would be back in a few minutes.

"And keep an eye on that pie in the oven. From the smell of the crust, it'll be done in a five minutes." Matilda ordered.

"*Danka*, Matilda." Eli said as they exited the bakery together. He shoved his thumbs through the straps of his suspenders and looked down at the ground. "Mollie was always good talking to the girls about things, but I have no idea what to say or to do."

"That's why I'm helping, Eli. I know how it is to be raising *kinner* on your own."

Betty sat miserably on the front bench of the buggy, arms wrapped around her middle tightly and eyes brimming with emotional tears. Her hazel eyes watched as Matilda approached the side of the buggy, and Betty scooted over to make room for Matilda to sit alongside her. Eli stood a few feet away to give them privacy.

"How are you feeling?" Matilda questioned gently.

"Horrible." Betty cried, hugging her middle more tightly." The cramping , it hurts so badly and everything else is just as bad."

Matilda wrapped a sympathetic arm around Betty's trembling shoulders. "I understand how horrible it feels, but I promise it will be better in time. Try some chamomile tea with honey when you get home and put a hot rag on your belly. That will help with the pain."

"Okay..." Betty said, and then turned to look at Matilda with a small wavering smile. "*Danka*, Matilda. I wish my *maemm* was here, but I'm happy you've been around to help us."

Tears stung the back of Matilda's eyes. While her *kinner* were skeptical of Eli's presence growing more frequent around their *haus*, his own *kinner* seemed to be willing to accept her. Her heart ached thinking of how terrifying it must have been for Betty when she realized she was coming into womanhood without her *maemm* around to help.

"Of course. I'm happy to have helped you."

She pressed a kiss to the top of Betty's prayer *kapp* and climbed out of the buggy to approach Eli.

"Stop by the store and grab her some chamomile tea and honey." Matilda told him. "That will help with the pain and let her rest for a couple of days."

"*Danka*, Matilda."

Eli smiled appreciatively, the softening of his eyes reminding her of the way hardened honey softens in the warm sunlight. He tipped his straw hat forward and started back towards his buggy. She lifted a hand in goodbye and watched them disappear around the corner before turning around to—

"Ach!"

Matilda's heart nearly leaped out of her ribcage to see Ryan standing motionlessly a few inches behind her. A Cheshire grin spread across his cleanly shaven face at catching her off guard and his eyes sparkled mischievously. Her knees weakened at his proximity. They were standing so close that her nose almost touched the center of his broad chest, and his cologne tantalized her senses again. The last time she had been this close to him had been the last night she spent with him at a park. Staring up at him, she could almost feel his lips on hers again and the memory warmed her face.

"I'm sorry. I didn't mean to startle you." he said, but his amused tone suggested otherwise.

Matilda cleared her throat and stepped back. She smoothed down the front of her dress even though it was wrinkle free and kept her gaze averted.

"How long were you standing there?" she asked.

"I don't know. Maybe a minute? I was walking around town and thought maybe my pie would be ready by now."

His pie! Matilda turned in panic to look back at the bakery, but didn't find smoke curling out the front door. She breathed out in relief. Lily had pulled it out on time.

"Yes, I'm sure it is. I'll go get it for you."

She rushed back to the bakery with Ryan following. All the while, Matilda prayed that *Gott* would help her find strength again. She opened the front door to find Rebecca standing behind the register with Lily and the till drawer opened as her *maemm* counted under her breath. Clearly annoyed, she stared at Matilda.

"There you are! Where have you— oh, hello." Rebecca stopped at the sight of Ryan entering behind Matilda. Matilda felt the flush deepen. "I suppose you're here for your pie. Lily, can you go get it please?"

Before Matilda could respond, Ryan brushed by her. He allowed the side of his arm to contact hers briefly, and it filled her with a fluttering heat. Ryan continued toward the counter confidently, flashing Rebecca a grin that showed off all his straight, white teeth.

"Yes, ma'am, and I have to tell you. Your pies are delicious. Better than any fancy baker in the whole United States."

Now it was Rebecca's turn to flush as she took in the compliment. "Oh, well. That's nice of you to say. Thank you for those kind words. I trust the wedding went well then?"

"Very much so." Ryan replied. "I told everyone there where all the pies came from., so I'd expect a boost in sales here soon."

For the first time in Matilda's life, she witnessed a flattered smile on her *maemm's* normally stern features. The smell of burnt pie crusts filled the air, and the door to the kitchen burst opened.

"I'm sorry!" Lily sobbed, covering her face in humiliation. "I forgot to take out the pie out and it's burned. Don't be mad Matilda—"

"I told you to take it out in five minutes!" Matilda said.

"I didn't think the Amish burned pies," Ryan said.

When they all turned to look back at him, he held up his hands. "I was just kidding. Like a joke. Ha ha."

Matilda bunched her fingers in the cotton fabric of her dress as a wave of grey smoke floated out into the bakery. Her *maemm* brushed by Lily and disappeared in the cloud of smoke.

"Wait." A strong grip on Matilda's elbow stopped her from rushing around the counter and after them. She glanced down at the circle of fingers around her elbow and then allowed her gaze to travel up the marooned sweater sleeve. Several emotions, too many to read fully, danced across the sharp features of his face. "I wanted to tell you something while people weren't around."

Matilda's heart thumped so loudly that she feared Ryan could hear it from the way he tilted his head. She felt the warmth from his fingers through the sleeve of her dress and his gentle strength from the way he held her arm. She looked down to his hand and swallowed thickly at the memory of those fingers brushing along her neck.

"What?"

"I wanted to tell you that I'm sorry about your husband. Your mom mentioned yesterday that you were raising your kids alone, and then the black dress made sense."

"Thank you," was all she could utter.

She really had no idea what to say. Curiosity finally got the better of her. "What are you still doing here?"

He frowned. "What am I still doing here?"

"*Ja.* What are you doing here still? The wedding is over."

"Relax. I'm not here to try to rekindle anything. I already know that wouldn't work from previous experience." He said, chuckling deeply. He shoved his hands in his front pockets and smiled assuredly at her. "I'm taking a bit of a vacation from my life, so to speak. I've been taking steps every day to get closer to God."

She played with the fabric of her apron. "That's, um, *gut?*" she said, uncertain of where this conversation would lead to. "I'm happy to hear that you have been taking steps to God."

"Yes, everyday. I have been looking at the Mennonite church for awhile now, but you know, the Amish lifestyle is way more appealing than anything else I've encountered."

Matilda had a hard time processing his words. What little bubble of safety she had around her silently popped and left her feeling exposed.

"You okay, Mattie? You look pale." Ryan said. He reached out to place a hand on her shoulder in concern and raised an eyebrow when she pointedly shrugged it away. "Did I say something—"

"Are you saying that you want to join the church?" she asked, knowing her voice revealed her disbelief.

"I'm saying that I've been thinking about it for a while now," Ryan corrected.

Matilda tried to imagine Ryan in their plain Amish clothing, living without the luxuries of an English life, devoting his life to Gott, and it didn't seem possible. Ryan had dismissed Gott so many years ago. What changed between then and now? The pulse of fear started underneath the weight of her shock. If he were serious about joining, which some part of her wanted to dismiss, it would mean he would be closer to her and to Rosella and the truth.

"It's-I-" She struggled to find her voice and form a coherent sentence. Finally she cleared her throat, and managed to talk. "I have to go. Lily will bake a new pie for you. Excuse me."

Naturally, curled eyelashes fanned the delicate skin under his eye when he winked slowly. The coy gesture brought her back to the first time he had winked at her when they first met; so incredibly calm, but flirty, and it had been alluring then. It was still alluring.

"I'll see you soon, then," he said, promise lacing his honeyed voice.

She fled before anything else could be said. In her rush to get away, Matilda failed to see Lily behind the kitchen door and barreled into her. They stumbled into the kitchen with oofs of pain.

"Ow!" Lily said, rubbing her head where Matilda's chin collided with. "I didn't think you were going to run through the door like that."

Matilda rubbed her own tender chin in irritation. "I didn't think you would be spying on me."

"Sorry. I couldn't help it." Lily said, shrugging her shoulders. "Does he want another pie or not?"

"He paid for one so I imagine he would want another pie."

"Don't get all crabby about it. What were you two talking about anyway that had you sprinting in here?"

"Nothing, Lily. Just please bake a pie for him." Matilda said, sighing in exasperation. "Where did *maemm* go?"

"Outside to throw away the— where are you going now?"

Matilda pushed the back door open and breathed in the crisp air with relief. She stumbled down the stairs on weak legs and began to fervently pray for strength. There was one thing she knew for sure at that moment:

Nothing made sense anymore.

CHAPTER SIX

The first breath of winter came sometime in the middle of the night. Matilda woke to a dry and scratchy throat, a dreaded sign of an oncoming cold. She moved about the *haus* quietly, relishing in the brief silence of the morning before her *kinner* awakened for morning prayers and started down the narrow steps that lead to the pantry.

She shivered at the cold air, wrapping her arms around herself, she walked down the neatly aligned shelves to where the tea leaves were stored. Her fingers brushed against the jar of Samuel's *kaffee*. Nine months later and she still could not bear the thought of throwing out his favorite drink. It was much like his clothes that still hung in their closet, still crisp and wrinkle free.

Yesterday lingered in the back of her mind. Ryan could not be serious about joining the Amish church. She refused to believe it from their previous exchanges on *Gott*. He had been the one to call the Amish judgmental towards the outsiders and even voiced his anger at her faith for not letting them be together past rumspringa. She did what she considered best at that moment—to push away what happened yesterday and force herself to not look any deeper into it. If not for her *kinner's* sake, for her own.

Matilda moved about the kitchen as she prepared her *kinner's* breakfast, scrambling a couple of eggs in a frying pan and slicing a couple of pieces of bread for them. She set a plate of butter in the middle of the table right as Rosella appeared in the doorway.

"Morning, Mama," she yawned out. "Do you need help with breakfast?"

"*Ja*. That would be lovely, Rose. Danka."

While Rosella supervised the scrambling eggs, occasionally scraping the frying pan, Matilda poured herself a cup of boiling water and added the dried mint leaves. She cradled the warm cup before inhaling the hot steam as the mint leaves steeped.

"Are you feeling sick again?"

At the panic quickly flooding Rosella's eyes, Matilda hurriedly set the cup down and rushed to assure her daughter.

"It's only a sore throat, Rosella. There's nothing to worry about it."

"That's what *daed* said, too."

Something twisted in Matilda, and it left a bitter taste in her mouth. She had been so consumed over the past nine months trying to figure out a way to survive without Samuel that she hadn't taken the time to realize how terrified her *kinner* were of losing her.

"That was a very different thing, Rose." Matilda said, cupping Rosella's jaw gently in the palm of her hand. "Listen to me, a cold will not kill me. It will take a lot more than that for me to be taken from this earth. Even if I have to fight *Gott* in staying here with you and your *bruders*. Understand?"

Tears clouded the sapphire eyes staring up at her before they were blinked away. Rosella gave a brief nod before slipping from Matilda's grasp and went to the cup of tea. She wordlessly handed it to Matilda before turning back to the stove.

"Don't worry, Mama. I'll take care of all the chores today while you go with Lily to get the fabric."

Matilda smiled genuinely at that. She sipped at her mint tea as Rosella busied herself in getting her *bruders* up and dressed before marching them down to breakfast. They bowed their heads in prayer before eating breakfast, and afterwards Matilda readied herself to go with Lily to the fabric store in town. All her *kinner* needed new clothes for the winter, especially her sons, and Lily agreed to help sew in exchange for her baking lessons.

"Behave, all of you." She said, kissing her boys on the tops of their head. "Mind your sister and if you need anything go straight to Almina next door."

Matthew wrinkled his nose in a grimace. "She always smells like cauliflower and cheese, Mama."

"Don't insult poor Almina." Rosella scolded, cuffing him on the back of his head.

"Do we really have to listen to Rosella, Mama?" Isaac chimed in. "She's really bossy."

Rosella puffed out her chest haughtily. "That's because I'm in charge when Mama's gone."

"All three of you get along please, for my sake." Matilda said, exasperated. "No fighting while I'm gone and if the three of you can't get along then I will have you all sit with Almina."

She hitched Pepper up to the buggy and cast one last glance in the direction of her *kinner*. They waved goodbye, but she didn't miss their glowering faces at being left behind with one another. Matilda bit back an amused laugh and continued down the road to pick Lily up.

The buggy treading forward in a soothing pull nearly lulled Matilda to sleep. She took in the colored leaves still clinging to the tree branches, and skirting along the road ahead of her. On their own accord, her thoughts strayed to first time Samuel had taken her for a ride in his buggy. She had nearly fallen asleep, cozily wrapped up in a thick blanket, and head resting on Samuel's sturdy shoulder. He had smelt like pine, and the forest after a chilly morning.

Matilda waited patiently outside her parent's *haus* for Lily to emerge. The front door opened, and her younger sister appeared with a scowling face. Lily climbed up into the buggy and she sullenly handed an envelope to Matilda.

"Ma says I have to give you this."

Matilda flipped the envelope open before closing it with a smile and slid it into the pocket of her dress.

"*Maemm* still doesn't trust you with money?" She inquired innocently.

Lily ignored her. Matilda steered the buggy back onto the main road. The steady clop of hooves filled the morning air as they road by fields and *hauses*.

"I keep telling her that I honestly didn't mean to lose the money. It fell out of my pocket on the way to the store."

"She knows that, Lily. Money's just too tight to be lost."

"I know, I know." Lily grumbled under her breath. She straightened suddenly and turned to look at Matilda in interest. "So, is Ryan really going to join our church?"

Matilda's gloved fingers tightened around the leather reigns. She kept her eyes focused ahead on the road as they approached town and tried to keep her emotions under control. Apparently, Lily overheard more of their conversation than she let on. Then again, Matilda didn't stay behind to see whether Ryan got his Whoopie pie.

"I don't know, Lily. I don't think so."

"Why not? He's thinking about joining the Mennonite church."

Matilda bit back an irritated sigh. Her throat had already begun to ache thinking of her conversation with Ryan yesterday and now with her sister's nosiness.

"That's a whole different thing, Lily. It would be easier for him to join the Mennonites if that's what he really wants."

"You sound like you don't think he wants to join."

"How many times have we've seen Englischers come in to our community and think that it'd be easier to live the way we do?"

"Quite a few times, I guess." Lily said thoughtfully. "So, you think he just said all those things because he's visiting."

Matilda nodded. "Exactly. I don't think he's serious."

That's what she forced herself to believe. Their lifestyle wasn't easy to adapt to or follow. It meant devoting your entire life to *Gott* and standing strong in His name and living true to His word. She was grateful to hear that *Gott* touched Ryan and brought him under His wing, but she doubted Ryan could ever commit to the church. Not after living his English lifestyle, and the Ryan she once knew.

They reached town a few minutes later and started down to the fabric store that Martha Lapp owned. For the next hour Matilda searched through the bundles of fabric, choosing simple colors and leaned against the counter as Martha cut the right amount of fabric she needed.

"How are you doing down at your *haus* all by yourself?" Martha asked kindly. Her delicate fingers folded a piece grey fabric neatly and placed it in the small pile on the counter.

"As *gut* as I possibly can be." Matilda replied, smiling. "How are all your *kinner*? Isaac has been asking to come over to your farm so he can play with John again in the creek."

Martha laughed softly. "Well, he is of course, welcome anytime. If you'd like some quiet time I'd be more than happy to watch your *kinner* and make sure they aren't getting into trouble..."

"Like last time?" Matilda added, laughing at the memory of poor Almina falling asleep on the couch only to realize that Matilda's *kinner* decided to play a game of hide and seek. She would never forget Almina riding in a panic to Eli's *haus*, where she had been helping Betty can vegetables, and informing her that her *kinner* were nowhere to be found. Matilda, well aware of their mischievous tendencies, found them sitting back at Almina's innocently when she returned to find them.

"Your *kinner* are well known for their pranks. Especially Rosella," Martha said.

"I know. She gets it from R—" Ryan. The word nearly slipped off her tongue freely and her dream from the previous night flashed inside of her mind sourly. "She gets it from Samuel, I mean."

"Really?" Martha arched an eyebrow in amusement. "I never saw Samuel as the pranking type. Not that I really know him that well. We courted only for a month."

Suddenly there was tension in the air. It wasn't a secret that Martha and Samuel had courted only for a month while Matilda was away on rumspringa, but it still didn't make it hurt any less or uncomfortable. She avoided Martha as much as she possibly could.

"I'm sorry," Martha said, a faint flush to her cheeks. "My mouth sometimes doesn't think things through."

"Don't worry about it. All is forgiven."

Matilda flashed her a smile and handed over the money needed to buy the fabric. She left the store a few minutes later with Lily close by her side and started in the direction of her buggy.

"Did you see the blue fabric?" Lily said, sighing dreamily. "I can't wait until I'm sewing my wedding dress."

"It'll happen before you know it." Matilda said, hugging the folded fabric against her chest as they rounded the corner of a building. "Let's head home before it gets colder and start on—"

They nearly collided with the two men rounding the corner simultaneously. Matilda quickly ducked her head in respect once she realized it was Bishop Abraham from his freckled cheeks and kind pale blue eyes.

"I'm sorry, Bishop. I wasn't paying attention to—"

She stopped in mid-sentence again except this time it was out of shock to see a familiar figure grinning at her from alongside Bishop Abraham. All at once her heart skipped a beat and plummeted to the balls of her feet. Her breath caught in her lungs until they burned for air; she couldn't hear for the blood pounding in her ears.

Ryan.

"Mattie" Ryan said, his grin growing wider. "Bishop Abraham was just showing me around Monte Vista and your community."

Matilda was speechless. In one second, her entire world was flipped upside down again, and this time Ryan was the source behind it. The emotions she had pushed aside earlier that morning came flooding back and overwhelmed her senses.

Abraham glanced at Matilda in surprise, no doubt at Ryan's use of the nickname, but if he was curious, he didn't venture to ask.

"You know our Matilda?" Bishop Abraham inquired, smiling warmly at her. He continued on, much to Matilda's relief, and spared them both an answer. "I have indeed been showing Mr. Myers around the community. He is exploring the idea of joining us."

The fabric fluttered down from Matilda's numb arms and onto the sidewalk. She could only stare at the two of them. The ground beneath her feet jerked back and forth rather violently and she teetered from the sensation.

"Matilda?" Lily called but her voice remained muffled from the pounding in Maitlda's head. "Are you are all right?" Lily asked. "You look like you are going to pass out. Is your cold getting worse?"

She felt someone touch her elbow. Aware of Bishop Mark's eyes watching her, Matilda shook her head free from its fuzziness and forced herself to remain still despite her skittering nerves.

"I'm fine. Maybe just a bit hungry. Let's go, Lily. It was nice seeing you again, Bishop."

She grabbed Lily and started down the sidewalk, dragging a bewildered Lily alongside her.

"Wait!" Ryan called out. "Hold on, Mattie. Wait a minute."

Matilda ducked her head and continued forward without glancing back. Hot tears clouded her vision as she continued to drag a squirming Lily alongside her. The logical part of her reasoned that this was juvenile and not in the Amish way to run away from someone. The other panicked part urged her legs to speed up before Ryan could catch up.

Lily finally managed wrenched herself free from Matilda's grip and they both came to a stop. "What is going on with you, Matilda? You dropped all the fabric and left it on the sidewalk."

"I—"

Footsteps pounded into the concrete behind them. Matilda edged around to see Ryan clutching the fabric she had dropped. Shame filled her for acting irrationally out of fear. This was not how an Amish woman behaved.

"You forgot these." Ryan said, offering her the unfolded fabric. When Matilda gingerly took the fabric from his arms, making sure not to touch him, he turned to Lily.

"Do you mind if I talk to your sister privately for a moment?"

Lily paused and looked at Matilda, uncertain what to do. At Matilda's tense nod, she shrugged and said she'd wait in the buggy.

Lily brushed by her, shooting her a pointed look before continuing down the sidewalk to give them their privacy. Matilda focused her attention on the task of brushing the fabric free from dirt and little rocks before folding them neatly against her chest. It gave her something to do and keep her from fidgeting.

"Mattie—"

"It's Matilda, Ryan. My name is Matilda here." She interrupted him, nearly dropping the fabric again from the tremble in her arms.

"Fine, Matilda. Could you please stop and look at me?"

She glanced at him, instantly regretting it a second later. Sunlight highlighted his sharp features and she knew if she wasn't careful she would easily lose herself in those soulful blue eyes. For that brief moment, she forgot about the rest of the world.

"Why don't you want me joining your church?" he asked plainly.

She bit her bottom lip until the metallic taste of blood filled her mouth. Was it fear? Or was it anger? Her soul battled to find which emotion to feel, but both emotions felt so deeply twined together that it was impossible to tell them apart.

"Why are you joining? The last time we were—"

"That doesn't matter anymore, Mattie." Ryan said, sighing in exasperation. He ignored the irritated look she gave him. "That was a long time ago. People change. People find God. People lose God. I'm not joining the church because of what we had. Yes, you were an inspiration to me for so many years. Maybe I need people like you in my life to keep me going the way I am? You have no idea what has happened in my life. I know that you've lost your husband and that you are trying to be strong for your family. You aren't the only person who lost someone they loved. Okay? I want to be closer to God, and this feels like it's the right way to be close to Him. My life is a constant headache of distractions, and I just want to be somewhere quiet where I can devote myself. Does that make sense?"

"I understand that, but—"

"But what? You don't want me to be here because of some reason and whatever that may be I'm saying don't worry about it." He paused for a moment, his jaw flexing as he chewed on the inside of his cheek. "Don't take this personally, but I really am not looking to join your community just to rekindle a brief relationship we had. I have a lot more respect for you than doing something like that. I just want to be closer to God."

The words were meant to be assuring, but it did the opposite. Even standing on the sidewalk an invisible rope tethered them together, and it squeezed around Matilda's waist tightly. It was hard to imagine the man standing in front of her being a part of her present and future when he had belonged in her past for so long.

The selfish part of her didn't want to see Ryan every day as a part of her community, to keep herself protected from the temptations Ryan brought out from her. It would open a door of intense emotions that Samuel had never been able to open. She loved Samuel with all her heart and still did, but that fiery sensation filling her always belonged to Ryan. Her thoughts trailed back to the dream and she grimaced inwardly. With only a couple of days, he had managed to rattle her in every way imaginable.

What would Samuel think? What would her *kinner* think?

Rosella's face danced in Matilda's mind. If she found out about the truth... She had done everything she could to protect Rosella, but now the past seemed insistent to play catch-up and she was helpless to guard her life from it.

Englischers strolled by and continued down the sidewalk towards the downtown section of Monte Vista. Leaves had fluttered down to the sidewalks in wet piles, and in the distance the rugged mountains were snow-capped. Grey clouds churned threateningly over the high terrain, and any day the cloud cover would reach the San Luis Valley.

Matilda avoided Ryan's gaze to hide the guilt she knew her eyes would reveal. Her Amish upbringing scolded her internally for turning away someone who needed spiritual guidance and who had come to her in friendship.

"If there's anything I can do to help let me know." Matilda said, forcing herself to look up at Ryan with a polite smile.

Ryan nodded and offered her a small smile in return. He reached out, his hand between them.

"I will, but until then, friends?"

She reached out tentatively and allowed her smaller palm to be enveloped in his. The calluses she remembered from years ago were still there on his finger tips. These were hands that were different from years of toiling work outside. They were different in their own strength. Warning bells in her mind professed that this was going to be a bad idea, but Matilda found herself agreeing with him. *Gott* surely would not bring Ryan back into her life for no reason, and wouldn't unless he thought she could handle it.

"*Ja.* Friends."

CHAPTER SEVEN

What little warmth the late fall offered during the days fell away when November graced the land. A chilled air greeted Matilda on Sunday when she stepped out into the early morning with her *kinner* following behind dutifully to complete their chores before visiting Matilda's parents.

"I'll race you." Matthew said to Isaac, giving him a playful shove.

The two took off towards the barn, their laughter breaking the dreariness of the over casted morning. Rosella stayed by Matilda's side, chewing on her bottom lip a bit apprehensively.

"Should you be outside, Mama?" Rosella asked suddenly. She raised worried eyes upwards to Matilda when she stifled a watery cough with a handkerchief. "I can handle all the chores and make sure everything gets done."

The sureness in Rosella's voice brought a proud smile to Matilda's face. Since her encounter with Ryan yesterday she had spent the majority of the night sitting in the rocking chair next to the wood stove, bent over a pair of trousers she needed to patch for Isaac. Her fingertips were well punctured from the needle tip by the time anxiety gave away to exhaustion. She woke to a sorer throat and a persistent watery cough.

"I'll be fine, Rosella. It's just a cold. Go ahead and milk the cows while I feed the chickens." Matilda said.

Rosella did as she was told without argument, grabbing a pail and little wooden bench. After checking on her son's chores of feeding the horses, Matilda filled her own pail with chicken feed and carefully danced around the squawking hens. She gathered warm eggs, placing them gently in a egg cartoon and then helped Matthew finish throwing hay over the stall doors to their cows.

While her *kinner* chatted happily on their way back to the *haus* Matilda coughed into her handkerchief and grimaced at the pain in her throat. When she did finally retire, she spent it by lying in the dark and hugging Samuel's pillow as she watched the shadows dance across the ceiling. Her conversation with Ryan played over in her mind.

"Why is he here *Gott*? Why now after so long?" she had whispered to the darkened room.

What was *Gott's* plan? She tried desperately to understand His reasoning behind it all. She could not dissuade Ryan from joining if that was *Gott's* plan for him, but why did it have to be her community specifically? It felt like a test and she prayed that she would make it through.

The questions still lingered in the back of her mind long after dawn broke and on their way to her parent's farm. Matilda spotted her *daed* in the field and lifted a hand in greeting when he looked in their direction. The second she pulled Pepper to a stop in front of the large barn, her *kinner* vaulted out of the buggy and sprinted towards Jonathan Beachey.

Rosella lingered briefly as Matilda led Pepper to the field to graze.

"Are you sure you're all right, Mama?"

Matilda smiled at her oldest, touched by her concern. "I will be fine." She flourished a shooing hand, "Now go on and play. You've had a long week of helping me out."

They shared a smile before Rosella disappeared around the corner of the barn to search for her *bruders*. Matilda's *maemm* was busy as usual in the small kitchen, pulling out a bubbling breakfast casserole from the oven when Matilda stepped in through the back porch door.

"Morning, Mama," Matilda said, unbuttoning her wool coat. She made sure to keep her handkerchief in the pocket of her dress. "Do you need help with anything?"

Rebecca placed the casserole in the center of the table with pot holders to cushion the dish and prevent it from burning the table. She dusted her hands, eyeing Matilda's red nose and watery eyes.

"*Nee*. I don't want you touching the food while you're sick. Lord knows nobody else can afford to be sick." She pulled out a chair, motioning for Matilda to sit down. "Now sit down and I'll make you some tea with honey."

"*Danka*, Mama."

The minute Rebecca disappeared through a door that lead to the pantry below the *haus* Lily emerged from the living room.

"It sounds like your cold got worse," Lily commented, sitting down in the chair across from Matilda.

"Really?" Matilda rolled her eyes, wiping at the edge of her nose in aggravation. "I didn't notice that it has gotten any worse."

"Don't be cranky. Where's Mama?"

"In the pantry."

Lily leant forward then and curiosity blazed in her eyes. "So is it true, then? Is Ryan really going to join our community? Is that what you two were talking about?"

There would be no point lying to Lily. She would figure it out somehow. Her sister had a rather annoying talent of sorting through gossip and finding the truth.

"He's thinking about it like I told you." Matilda said.

"That's what he wanted to talk to you about yesterday?"

"*Ja*, Lily. That was all we talked about." Matilda said, rubbing at her eyes wearily. Their *maemm's* footsteps in the hallway ended their brief conversation. Rebecca entered the kitchen with a jar of tea leaves and a jar of honey as well. She glanced over at Lily sitting innocently across from an apprehensive Matilda and slowly set the items down on the kitchen counter.

"Could you go fetch everyone for breakfast?" Rebecca asked Lily.

It really wasn't a question, but Lily did as she was told by wordlessly leaving the two of them alone in the kitchen.

Matilda picked nervously at a random splinter in the table top. She winced when it finally came loose and embedded itself in the pad of her finger. Her *maemm* knew something was going on from the knowing gaze that she currently fixated on her.

"Is it true that Englischer Ryan is thinking about joining our community?"

"You heard what we were talking about?"

Her *maemm* merely sniffed and started to boil some water for Matilda's tea.

"Of course I did." She said, setting glasses down on the table. "This is my *haus* after all. I know what's being said in these walls."

Matilda smiled thinly. She remembered that statement well throughout her childhood and teenage years. At first Matilda believed it to be a empty threat, but after several occasions of being caught red-handed she realized quickly her *maemm* did have the uncanny ability to figure things out.

None of that helped with her nerves churning inside with such force that it made her stomach heave.

"Well?" Rebecca prompted when no answer came.

"He's thinking about joining." Matilda replied, keeping her voice steady as possible. "He has been talking to Bishop Abraham about joining, as well as talking to the Mennonite church."

The smell of mint leaves and honey filled the kitchen. Rebecca set the steaming mug down in front of Matilda and then placed a loaf of bread next to the breakfast casserole.

"It makes sense now," she said, sweeping around the kitchen with ease and familiarity. "I mean, why you are sick from nerves and why he has been around the bakery every day."

Matilda felt the blush as she met her *maemm's* stare. She focused on the pad of her throbbing finger and tried to push out the tiny sliver of wood from her skin.

"I just have a cold. It has nothing to do with Ryan." she said.

"Right," Rebecca replied wryly. "You think I don't notice things, do you? You may be a grown woman and a *maemm* yourself, but you are still my daughter. I know when something is bothering you and the last time you were sick was shortly after Samuel died."

She opened her mouth to defend herself, but Rebecca continued on. "I know that your sister seems to think that Ryan is here because of you and I share the same opinion. I don't know how you know that Englischer and nor does it matter for me to know now. For the sake of your *kinner* don't let yourself get close to him. Not when you have someone like Eli who would be a better father figure."

You don't know that, *maemm*. You don't know what type of father he would be.

The urge to argue crawled beneath Matilda's clammy skin. She curled her fingers into fists and sought control of her rapidly fraying temper.

"Why are you telling me all this?" Matilda asked. "That decision would be mine to make once that time is before me. Not yours."

"You're right. It's your decision, but I'm only trying to help. You're my daughter and I love you. I just worry about your heart being broken again."

Matilda didn't reply. Her shame for being confrontational towards her *maemm* when she was only trying to help her avoid heartache silenced her. She would do the same thing for Rosella in a heartbeat if it meant protecting her oldest *kinner* from any pain.

"I know, Mama. I'm sorry. You don't have to worry about me."

"*Gut*. Lord knows I have enough to worry about."

The next morning Matilda's throat ached even more. No amount of tea or honey seemed to soothe it. Tired of her coughing, but also concerned, Rebecca relieved Matilda from the rest of her duties at the bakery. Something that did not go unnoticed by Lily who scowled moodily at being ordered to take on Matilda's responsibilities.

Matilda dabbed at the wetness in her nose as she slipped out through the front of the bakery. She rounded the corner and started towards the direction of the general store to purchase more tea, but found Eli coming from the same direction.

"I have something that I thought you might need." Eli said, smiling.

He held out a box of mint tea leaves and a bottle of honey. Matilda took the items with a small grateful smile. Her bad mood lessened greatly at the touching gesture.

"*Danka*, Eli." Matilda said. "I really needed these things today. Why aren't you at your construction job?"

"I'm on the way, but your *maemm* told me when I was buying a pastry that you were ill with a cold. So I thought I'd buy these as a thank you for helping out with Betty."

"There's no need to thank me. Any of us in the community would have helped."

"*Ja*, but not the way you helped. You've got a way with helping people."

Matilda ducked her head bashfully at the compliment and then felt her nose dripping again. Mortified, Matilda wiped hastily at her nose and prayed that Eli didn't see it.

"You better get home and get some rest," Eli said.

He took a timid step forward and then grabbed Matilda's hand in a soft squeeze. She tried not to tense up at the contact, her heart leaping, and their eyes meet when Eli stepped back. His eyes were softened once again.

"I'll check up on you if you'd like after work. See if you need anything else?"

"*Ja.* That'll be fine."

He left her then to stand on the sidewalk, watching him retreat back in the same direction he came from. Matilda looked down at the items in her hands and a headache pounded at the back of her head. Maybe her *maemm* was right. Choosing Eli would be the best choice for herself and for her *kinner's* lives. He was home, he was their community, he was everything that Matilda believed in. Until that point, she had only known the collected side of Eli and seldom witnessed the caring side. On the occasions that she did witness the caring side, it never ceased to make her feel special or like she had been the only one he was thinking about. No one would be able to replace Samuel in their hearts, but she couldn't keep going at the pace she was going. She couldn't afford to fall gravely ill.

A tall shadow appeared next to hers on the sidewalk. Matilda looked over her shoulder to where Ryan stood behind her, hands shoved casually in the front pocket of his jeans. His initial grin faded away to concern once he took in her red nose and miserable expression.

"You look like terrible," Ryan said.

Matilda scoffed out a sarcastic laugh. "*Danka,* Ryan. That's really nice of you to point out the obvious."

"Ouch. Someone's a bit cranky today."

She bit her bottom lip to contain the immediate reply on the tip of her tongue. *Ja*, I'm cranky because I'm tired of you haunting my dreams and not staying in the past where you belong.

"I don't have time for this, Ryan," Matilda said tightly. "If you excuse me, I don't feel well and I need to get home—"

Ryan stepped in her line of path and held out his hands in surrender. He then dug out his car keys and jingled them at her.

"Let me drive you home. You look sick and it's cold out."

She blanched at the thought of driving in a car with Ryan. What would her community and family think then? Driving around a car with a Englischer? Not a good idea. The last time she rode in a car was the first night their community doctor decided it would be best to take a wheezing Samuel to the hospital. They tried to stay with their community doctor for a natural way to recover from his sickness, but it became clear very fast after coughing up blood that he needed help from the English doctors. By then it had been too late.

"I'm sorry," Ryan started apologetically. "I didn't think-"

"It's okay," Matilda said, shaking her head politely. "*Danka* for the offer, but I have to take Pepper home and the buggy as well."

"Are you sure?"

Matilda shifted on her feet, and tried to think of the gentlest way to explain the Amish view of cars. It was clear that he still hadn't given up all the luxuries of an English life.

"Yes, I'm sure. We Amish don't drive in cars unless it is an emergency, and I doubt that this is an emergency."

"Okay. I get what you're saying. You can't be seen in a car. Well, I'll walk with you then to your, em, buggy." His brows furrowed at the word, but he gestured for Matilda to continue walking.

Matilda walked down the sidewalk in resignation to the field where they kept their horses and buggies. She wanted to go home, enjoy the silence of her *haus* and take a long needed nap before having to rise and gather her *kinner* from school. The wood stove would fight away the chilly air and the surrounding grayness of the approaching winter. Several of the fields alongside the business and the park where English children played were beginning to fade into a dull color of yellow. Still, Matilda found herself in awe of how the seasons changed before her, and how she changed with them. When Samuel had passed away to Heaven, it had been March and spring was upon them. The seasons continued on like he had never left, and a surreal thought crossed Matilda's mind when she glanced over at Ryan. How strange was it to be next to someone as the fall chilled away to winter?

They passed the general store and neared the open field where horses grazed. Matilda tried not to breathe in the crisp air too much, her lungs already burning from the chill. For a brief moment, she felt what Samuel described how his lungs felt to her. Like I'm breathing fuel and flames, he'd said. Matilda shivered at the sensation.

"So, may I ask you something now that we are friends?" Ryan asked.

She glanced up at him, his long jean legs keeping stride with her easily. She debated telling him no, that she just wanted to walk in silence, but nodded her head.

"I hope you don't mind me asking, but how did your husband die?"

Matilda stopped walking a few yards shy of the field in surprise at the question. "You want to know how my husband died?"

"I know that it's a weird question to ask," Ryan said, reading her thoughts perfectly, "but I have a reason why I'm asking you. You don't have to tell me if it's really that painful, but I swear there is a reason why I'm asking."

"This—" Matilda started, fidgeting with her damp handkerchief. This isn't right. "Why are you so curious about how my husband died?"

"I have a reason for asking, but if this is how you want to do things then I have no problem talking first."

He pointed to one of the many wooden benches around Monte Vista's downtown. Matilda sat down on the edge, smoothing out the skirts of her dress and tried not to bounce her legs anxiously as Ryan situated himself next to her with a couple feet of space between them. They watched as Englischers walked slowly down the sidewalks, peering into the shop windows as they passed by. The faint smell of cinnamon and apple filled the chilly air while the sun disappeared behind a thick blanket of clouds. The trees lining the sidewalks rustled in the wind and the remaining fiery red leaves rained down on them.

"I know you're a bit confused about why I really am looking to join the Amish church, particularly your community, but there really is a benign reason." Ryan paused briefly, leaning forward to rest his elbows on his knees. "My mom was diagnosed with stage four breast cancer four years ago. By the time they found the lumps it was pretty much too late and my mom decided to go on God's will, as she would say. She asked me to pray with her all the time and take her to church. I did it at first to humor her, but I kept thinking "Why would God allow someone like my mom be diagnosed with something like that?" And after she died, I just kept going to church somehow and I brought my sister with me to give her some guidance."

A group of Englischer's passed by them, gazing at Matilda's curiously as they continued down the sidewalk and towards the downtown businesses. The chilly breeze stirred the strands of Matilda's hair from underneath her *kapp* and she wiped at her nose as discreetly as possible. Her heart softened slightly hearing about Ryan's mother passing away from sickness. In a way, it made her feel even more connected to him thinking of Samuel's death.

"I'm sorry to hear about your mother," she said, and she truly was sorry. "I know how hard it is to lose someone that you love and find solace in *Gott*."

Ryan gave a shake of his fair head. "I wouldn't say I found solace in God right away. I was actually pretty angry with God after she died. I didn't understand why He would take my mom of all people."

Matilda bit her bottom lip. She had asked *Gott* the same thing more than once, but then comforted herself by thinking of Samuel in Heaven.

"I, too, asked *Gott* about Samuel, but then I remember that death brought him to *Gott* and he is happy in Heaven."

"You really believe that?" He didn't look confrontational or dubious, just merely curious.

"*Ja.* Of course I do. What else is there to believe in?"

"Nothing. You're right about that."

They shared a hesitant smile. Ryan rested his cheek against his laced hands and studied Matilda intently with a small smile.

"I wish I was more like you," he said wistfully. "I really have missed you, Mattie. I hope we can be friends."

"I'm sure we can be friends if you join," Matilda said.

"That sounds like a big if doesn't it?" Ryan chuckled deeply, his white teeth flashing quickly. "Bishop Mark is willing to let me attend a church service this upcoming Sunday. Even gave me some clothes to wear so I will blend in a bit easier."

Matilda doubted he would ever blend in fully. A new face and coupled with attractive looks was sure to gain him attention from the single women in her community. Jealousy smoldered inside of her much to her horror and surprise.

"I doubt that you will blend in," Matilda said. She cleared her throat and grimaced at the hot pain climbing up her throat. "I'm sorry, Ryan, but I really need to get home. I am not feeling well."

"Of course. I'm sorry. I took up more time than I should have."

He stood up quickly, offering a hand for Matilda to take. She hesitated for a moment, but then slowly placed her smaller palm in the center of his. Fingers clasped around hers gently and then tugged her upwards easily. Her arm felt like it was aflame from the simple touch. Much to her relief, Ryan let go of her hand and they started back towards the field again.

"You never told me what happened to Samuel," Ryan said. At her surprised look, he clarified, "That was our agreement. I tell you what brought me to *Gott* and you tell me what happened to you."

A shiver bubbled its way up Matilda's spine at the sound of Ryan's syrupy voice slipping into Pennsylvania Dutch. She could only imagine how the rest of the Amish language would sound coming from Ryan's tongue. Maybe it wasn't such a bad idea to have him join the community. She wouldn't ever tire hearing it.

Her heart swelled in alarm at that internal admission. What was wrong with her? Matilda prayed for strength then to resist any other tempting thoughts beginning to cloud her mind.

"Why do you want to know?" she croaked out.

Ryan arched a golden eyebrow. "I thought that would be obvious. I know what it's like to lose someone. so I thought it'd be good for our friendship to share things like that."

They reached the field where various buggies were parked in front of a wooden gate. Matilda set the box of tea leaves and a jar of honey inside the buggy and turned to look at Ryan thoughtfully. What would the difference be telling Ryan than telling Eli?

"He died from pneumonia nine months ago," Matilda said, her voice grown soft. Tears immediately obscured her vision and she looked down at the ground to hide them. "We tried everything we could to fight it, but the English doctor at the hospital told us that the pneumonia he had was from a bacterial infection and at that point it was already too late. No drugs or anything could stop the damage."

They were silent for a while besides the whisper of a wind in the dry grassy field and horse hooves stomping along the dirt. Once Matilda managed to regain control over herself, she looked up and met Ryan's sympathetic eyes.

"I'm sorry, Mattie. I do know how it feels to feel helpless when there is nothing you can do anymore. It's exhausting afterwards and it takes time to heal."

Matilda wiped her eyes dry with the sleeve of her wool coat. She nodded her head in agreement.

"Exactly. That is how it feels, but *Gott* will get me through this. I know it."

"I really wish I was like you, Mattie." Ryan repeated again, a deep sadness filling his voice. "I still feel so guilty for what has happened that it's hard to sleep at night anymore."

"Over your mother's death?"

"That too, but—" He paused to take a deep and steadying breath, his broad shoulders moving with the action. "There was something else that made me realize I need to find God in my life. I became a person that I'm not proud of. My business sky rocketed, but it made me greedy and I did something that I don't know if I'll ever truly forgive myself for."

Matilda's heart thundered at the tormented expression displayed on Ryan's face. He truly appeared to be in emotional pain from the tears that glistened in his eyes when they looked into hers hauntingly.

"I had to fire a man who'd been with me from day one in building up my company. There were rumors going around the office that he was taking money or someone close to me was. So, I fired all of them. A week later his wife called me and said that he had killed himself because he was unable to deal with the stress of not knowing how they were going to support their family. Later I found out it was another employee who was taking chunks of money and overcharging companies. I realized after that how bad of a person I had become and I wanted to change."

"I'm sorry." she said.

Her heart ached thinking of how money seemed to ruin lives and force people to do things they normally wouldn't do. Ryan was no exception to the temptation of money and he paid the consequences for it. She reached toward him and placed her hand on the upper of his chest. The softness of his sweater felt good underneath her finger tips. He exhaled loudly, turning his head to look at her hand. This had to be the reason why *Gott* pulled them together; she thought, for her to help him spiritually.

"You're doing the right thing by being here," Matilda said confidently. "*Gott* has already forgiven you if you are willing to forgive yourself."

"I hope that I can in time."

CHAPTER EIGHT

The next morning Matilda rose early again. She braved the cold by gathering more chopped wood and added the chilled chunks to the smoldering charcoal remains inside the wood stove. She kept the door cracked open, as Samuel had shown her, to create a draft and fuel the fire. Once a fire roared back to life she shut the doors firmly and adjusted the metal knobs on the front before sitting down in her rocking chair, Samuel's <u>Ausband</u> cracked open on her lap.

And lead us not into temptation.

Matilda stared down at the scripture, repeating it several times in her mind until she could gather some sort of composure and strength. She slept fitfully all night thinking of church and how Ryan would be there as part of the testing period. She took a deep breath, sweating slightly from the waves of heat now coming from the wood stove.

She leaned her head back against the rocking chair and reached up to twirl a piece of hair around her finger.

"*Gott,* what should I do?"

Her thoughts wandered to a memory that replayed over inside her mind.

"Those English boys are looking at us," Lucy said.

She stood confidently in the middle of the aisle filled with books, dressed in an English summer dress that complemented her slender body perfectly and cradling a cup of

Starbucks coffee. Her dark hair hung around her waves in smooth curly waves, and dimples formed in the center of her cheeks.

Matilda kept her back turned to the boys. She could feel their eyes focused intently on them and the hair on her arms stood on edge from the sensation. The summer dress that Lucy lent her felt suddenly too tight against her breasts and too short as the fabric brushed against the middle of her thighs. She reached up to twirl a piece of hair around her finger, something she did whenever she was nervous.

"We should go." Matilda said. "Let's go to the mall and—"

"Hold your horses, Matilda. Let's talk to them."

Lucy wound an arm through Matilda's before she could protest and turned her around. A tall young man with honey-blonde hair, two years older she guessed, and the darkest pools of blue for eyes stood further down the aisle. He leaned his muscular frame casually against the bookcase, shooting a friendly smile in Matilda's direction as she was dragged by Lucy down the aisle.

Her heart pounded so hard that it would surely burst through her chest. Matilda timidly raised her eyes to sapphire eyes looking down at her with a confident smile curling his lips. A strange feeling coursed through her body and it left her shaky and exhilarated all at once. She knew right then and there he was a temptation.

"Hi. My name is Lucy, and this is my friend, Matilda,"Lucy said as she stared at the man with brown hair. "We're new around here and we were just wondering what we could do."

Lucy batted her newly mascaraed eyelashes. She tightened her twined arm to keep Matilda firmly at her side.

"Pleasure, Lucy, Matilda. I'm Max." The brown-haired man grinned. "This hjere's my best friend since kindergarten, Ryan. Ryan Myers."

Ryan.

His name echoed inside her mind. It felt right, lingering on the tip of her tongue. Matilda blushed at the thought and ducked her head to hide her embarrassment. Since when was she so shy in front of boys? Her whole community back in Lancaster was full of them, and she interacted with them every day at her *maemm's* bakery.

"So, where are you ladies from?" Max asked.

"Lancaster, PA." Lucy replied casually. "We are visiting my aunt for the summer."

"Lancaster?" Ryan echoed. "I don't mean to be rude or whatever, but isn't that where the Amish are from?"

Matilda caught the warning in Lucy's eyes. She hesitated in answering, not wanting to lie to the first English boy who talked to her on rumspringa.

"How would you know that, dude?" Max asked then, sparring them from answering. "I don't even honestly know where Pennsylvania is at that moment."

Ryan tilted his head towards Max. A mischievous glint filled his sapphire eyes as sunlight streaming through the glass windows haloed him. The coziness of the setting sun and music playing soft in the store eased a little tension churning in Matilda's stomach.

"Because, Max, I'm taking a religion course and we've talked about the Amish. It's called educating yourself," Ryan said.

"Ha ha," Max said, rolling his eyes. "How about this? Amish or not, we'll show you around Denver. We're good guys, I promise."

Lucy didn't consult Matilda for an answer. She nodded eagerly, letting go of Matilda's arm, and seizing onto Max's offered arm instead. Matilda watched her best friend bat her eyelashes demurely up at Max as the two of them started down the aisle.

This was what rumspringa was about; doing things that they wouldn't normally do in their community. Matilda's stomach tightened in nervousness thinking of all the rules they would undoubtedly break this summer. In Lucy's case that meant talking to a cute English boy and allowing him to escort her around the city while dressed in a rather flimsy summer dress.

"So," Ryan said, still not moving from where he leaned against the bookshelves, "Are you really Amish? You look like a deer in the headlights."

"A deer in the what?"

"It's just a saying. You must be Amish."

Matilda tried to avoid his look. Not that she was ashamed of her background, but because he seemed to be able to read her too well.

"I am," she said softly. "Is that going to be a problem?"

"Why would it be?"

Matilda returned from the memory before it could go any further. Their meeting had been a huge problem then. How did things turnaround so fast?

She watched as the morning sun finally made an appearance in the sky. A pale blue light tumbled in through the windows and in the distance a rooster crowed. She continued to recline back in the chair, rocking backing and forth at a soothing pace. At some point exhaustion took over and she fell into a hot fitful sleep.

"Mama?"

Matilda jerked awake. She straightened, rubbing at the fuzziness still clouding her eyes. She couldn't remember what she had been dreaming, but she still wanted to clutch onto it.

A white cotton nightgown with blonde hair cascading freely around small shoulders brought Matilda's attention to Rosella standing in front of her. Knobby knees and long gangly arms, Rosella was every bit of a child forming into a young woman.

"What time is it?" Matilda asked, easing herself up into a standing position. "Are your *bruders* awake?"

Rosella gave a shake of her head.

"*Nee*. They aren't awake yet, but it's almost 8:30 and—"

"It's almost 8:30?" Matilda bolted out of the rocking chair, ignoring her body's grimace at the sudden movement. "Go upstairs and get ready. If we're lucky we can make it to church without being too late."

Matilda managed to gather her *kinner* promptly and made sure they all were presentable for church. She clucked at Pepper to pick up the pace as they trotted down the road in the direction of the Byler *hause* where church would be held today. They huddled together under the thick blanket in their buggy against the chilly morning air that would only warm a couple degrees. With each hoofbeat closer to where Ryan would be, the harder Matilda's heart hammered within her chest. The calmness she had somehow gathered earlier crumbled.

There was no doubt in her mind that church would be interesting today with Ryan sitting with the *mensleit*.

Matilda picked at the bowl of cheese salad she made for lunch after church concluded. She waited for Almina to set down her own contribution, various baked breads that went perfectly with Matilda's cheese salad, on the kitchen counter in the Byler's *haus*. Today they were taking shifts since it was too cold to hold church in the barns and Matilda belonged to the second one.

She emerged from the crowded kitchen to the equally crowded living room where furniture was arranged to seat everyone comfortably. Matilda scanned the sea of prayer *kapps* and black hats, but found no sight of Ryan anywhere. A small part of her deflated in disappointment while the other part of her breathed out in relief. At least she could enjoy today's hymns and sermons without focusing on Ryan somewhere in the crowd.

Eli managed to squeeze through the crowded living room to Matilda's side. "You are looking much better this morning. Are you feeling better?"

"*Ja*. Much better. *Danka* for getting the tea and honey. I haven't had a chance to thank you all week."

"No need to thank me. I was just trying to help you out since you've helped us out."

Matilda smiled warmly. "You've helped us out just as much with all the farm work and upkeep that you help me with."

He dug the toe of his boot into the floorboards in a bashful gesture. Matilda played with the edge of her apron, unsure of what to say or do.

"Matilda, I—" Eli started, but cut off suddenly.

His hazel eyes were focused on something behind her and a puzzled expression spread across his face. Before she could turn to see what caught his attention, a familiar syrupy voice washed over her.

"Hi, Mattie."

Her heart would surely burst from how frantically it pumped! Of all the three shifts they had today for church, Ryan had to be at the one she attended with not only her family, but her *kinner* as well. Matilda twirled her fingers anxiously in the fabric of her apron as she slowly turned around to face him and immediately regretted it.

Gone were his Englischer's clothes. Ryan stood tall dressed in a cleanly pressed white button up shirt, black trousers with suspenders, and leather boots. A black hat was perched on honey blonde locks and his sapphire eyes sparkled at her mischievously.

"How do I look?" he asked, flourishing at his clothes. "Do I look Amish now?"

"*Ja*," she said, and blushed at how hoarse her voice sounded. "You will blend in better now that you aren't in your English clothes."

Ryan grinned, clearly pleased to have Matilda's approval. She had never thought she would live to see Ryan in Amish clothes or trying to join her community. They continued to stare at one another until Eli cleared his throat pointedly and Matilda broke it off.

"Ach, I'm sorry, Eli." Matilda turned around to introduce the two of them. "Eli, this is Ryan. He is hoping to join our community."

A tense moment followed. Eli slowly extended his hand while offering a tense but polite. smile.

"*Wunderbar* to hear. I hope *Gott* will help you through your journey to joining our church."

"Thank you," Ryan said, nodding his head. "I hope that as well. Mattie, could we tal—"

"Church is about to start," Eli interrupted, nodding to the living room. "We better go find our seats, Matilda."

Eli placed a hand on Matilda's lower back and ushered her foreword. She tensed at the contact and shrugged away from his hand. The whole time she felt Ryan's eyes on them and the hair on the back of her neck stood on edge from being watched.

After seating Isaac and Matthew alongside her *daed*, Matilda sat down on a little wooden bench between her *maemm* and Rosella. As the room filled with singing hymns and Minister Larry's smooth voice, she kept herself focused on the sermons. This was *Gott's* time with her. She would have plenty of time to focus on other matters later. A wave of calm settled on Matilda's shoulders as they began to pray. No matter how stressed she was. attending church always created a bubble of contentment for her. There was nothing better than feeling *Gott's* presence in the room.

An hour later church concluded early for more time to have Fellowship. From the corner of the room Matilda watched as Minister Larry talked with Ryan, occasionally letting out a jovial laugh and introducing him to whoever walked up to them. Ryan's appearance created quite the stir within their Amish community, especially with the women.

Their excited buzz and whispers over "how handsome" Ryan was filled Matilda's ears as she picked moodily at her plate of food.

"Isn't he handsome?" Lily whispered to the group of women who had gathered around Matilda. At their exaggerated nods, she smirked victoriously. "I told you that he was handsome. He's friends with Matilda."

Matilda clenched her teeth. Several of the women swiveled to look at her.

"You know the Englischer, Matilda?" Katie Miller asked.

"Is he single, Matilda?"

"Can you mention my name?"

"Ladies," Martha broke in, holding up her hands to silence the slew of excited questions, "I think the better question to ask is how did Matilda strike up such a close friendship with him? The whole time during service he didn't take his eyes off her for very long."

Her heart flipped at that observation. He was watching her the whole time? Matilda cleared her throat and schooled her features into a neutral look.

"I think you ladies are making it out to be a bigger deal than what it is. We're not really close friends."

Martha scoffed loudly. "I don't think so, Matilda. From what I hear, he's been hanging around your maemm's bakery every day."

"And so has Eli." Katie put in. "I've seen him visiting every other day."

"My maemm's baking brings several mensleit in. There's not anything different going on," Matilda said defensively.

A headache began to pound in her temples. The living room felt too hot and stuffy all of a sudden from the wood stove and the nosy women. She had no idea why they were idling in such petty gossip, but apparently Ryan brought out that in people. Some part of her didn't blame them though for being curious over his sudden appearance and interest in joining their community.

"Even if there is or isn't," Martha said, flipping the string of her kapp out of her face, "I wouldn't let this one pass by. Not that there is anything wrong with Eli, but if I weren't married..."

She trailed off with a dreamy giggle. Matilda stabbed a piece of fruit with more force than necessary and then set the fork down, surprised by the jealousy burning in her.

"Excuse me ladies," Matilda said, setting the plate down on the table, "I have to check on my *kinner* and get some fresh air."

Matilda left the group before anything else could be said. She searched through the living room for any sight of her *kinner* and found them sitting alongside her parents. She was thankful then that they had been sitting with her parents instead of listening to all those questions.

"Matilda?"

With one arm stuck in the sleeve of her coat, Matilda turned to see Eli walking down the narrow hallway in her direction. She groaned inwardly, thinking of the conversation that just went on. She didn't want to add any more fuel to the fire.

"I'm just going outside for some fresh air," she said and opened the front door. "I'll be back in a few minutes."

"Do you want me—"

She shut the door before Eli could finish his question. The cold air felt good on her warm skin as she walked around the porch that wrapped about the house.

Matilda grasped the porch railing and took several large breaths to stabilize herself. She focused on the horses grazing in the field across from her and the chickens clucking nearby until the tension eased from her muscles.

"It's really peaceful out here."

Her feet nearly left the floorboards at the adrenaline shooting through her veins at the sound of Ryan's voice. She whirled around, clutching at her frantically beating heart.

"You scared me," she accused breathily. "Don't sneak up on people like that."

Ryan shrugged his shoulders apologetically. "I wasn't sneaking up on you. I came outside to get some fresh air and saw you standing over here by yourself."

"*Ja.* I needed some fresh air too."

They stood side by side on the porch. She found herself looking him over. It seemed impossible that even dressed in plain clothing Ryan still looked incredibly handsome. She leaned back against the porch railing to put some distance between them.

"How did you like the sermons?" Matilda asked.

"They were good. The only problem is that I didn't understand a word whenever everyone started singing. Maybe you could help me learn the language? I remember little from what you told me so many years ago."

Martha's words echoed in Matilda's mind. She hesitated, not wanting to draw more attention to herself by being around Ryan.

"I'm sure you can find someone else to teach you. Minister Larry could probably give you a lesson."

"I'd rather it come from you."

There it was again. The simplest of phrases that weakened Matilda's knees and it took all her restraint not to swoon. This was ridiculous, she scolded herself. Her attraction for Ryan couldn't possibly be that strong to feel the way she did. They were only friends and would remain that way. If Ryan didn't survive the testing period or decided that living by the *Ordnung* wasn't for him, what then?

Before Matilda could reply, Minister Larry appeared around the corner of the haus and beckoned Ryan over to him.

"Excuse me, Matilda," he said, smiling warmly at her. "I need to borrow Ryan for a few more introductions and talk some more."

"I'll see you around," Ryan told her, winking again.

Matilda watched him disappear around the corner and drummed her hands in irritation on the porch railing. She sometimes swore that Ryan said certain things on purpose to rattle her.

The afternoon finally gave away to the sun beginning its descent down to the west horizon. For the rest of the time she spent at the Byler *haus*, Matilda managed to avoid any direct conversation with Eli or Ryan. After gathering her *kinner* and tucking a blanket around their legs to fight off the cold, Matilda gladly steered their buggy back in the direction of their *haus*.

Rosella sat alongside her quietly for some time, before turning to look at Matilda.

"How do you know Ryan? I mean, everyone was talking about how he seemed to be attracted to you more than anyone else."

"It's complicated, Rosella," Matida replied stiffly.

"What's complicated about it?"

"Rosella," Matilda started with an exasperated sigh, her stomach twisting into so many painful knots that it was hard to breath, "It just is. Some things are complicated in life. You'll understand once you get a bit older."

"I'm fourteen, *maemm*," Rosella said, rolling her eyes dramatically. "I know all about complicated things."

Matilda let out a full-bellied laugh despite her irritated mood. "I'm sure you do, Rosella. I'm sure you do."

CHAPTER NINE

The last bit of fiery reds covering the mountainsides faded away to a dull brown and patches of white now tagged the rugged mountain tops. Grey clouds loomed and they would tumble down from the high peaks to the valley. It was only a matter of time before the snow would come down, and it was something they all waited for anxiously. One day they would wake up to fluffy flakes of white snow sprinkling down on the like *Gott* was dusting flour on a counter.

"Who is that rhubarb crisp for?"

Matilda looked up from sprinkling the top of rhubarb with crumbled pieces of oats and melted butter. She rolled her eyes at the mischievous smile on Lily's face.

"It's not for Ryan. If that's what you're wondering."

"Who's it for then?"

"Why does it matter?"

"Because I'm curious.""

"It's not for Ryan. You know he only orders Whoopie pies," Matilda insisted with an exasperated sigh. "It's for an Englischer. She'll be here in the next hour or so to pick it up."

"What about Ryan's pie?"

"Honestly, Lily. What about it?"

Lily danced around the kitchen island that was cluttered with bowls and spatulas. She practically glued herself to

Matilda's side and followed her about the kitchen as they finished baking the last couple of apple butter pies. The smell of cinnamon and butter filled the tiny kitchen.

"Doesn't he pick one up every day now or is that just an excuse to see you?" Lily asked.

"Don't start on that. I'm tired of hearing it from everyone else."

"You hear it because it's true. I don't think he's joining for spiritual reasons entirely. *Maemm* thinks the same thing too, but she isn't so open to you marrying—"

"I'm not marrying anyone!" Matilda cut in sharply. "He's joining to be closer to *Gott*; not because of me."

At that moment, Matilda was glad that in a few short weeks Lily would turn sixteen and be distracted with rumspringa. She shoved the crisp in the oven and washed her fingers free from the clumps of oats sticking to them. This is what she feared with Ryan being around and insisting on being friends. Church confirmed what the community thought of Ryan's reasons for joining or at least the women's opinions of why he wanted to join.

Her courtship with Samuel had been private and their marriage as well. They certainly didn't attract this much attention from the community, and the constant flow of questions wore on Matilda's irritated nerves. She had enough to deal with around the *haus* and raising her *kinner* to the best of her ability.

"How's *daed* doing?" Matilda asked, changing the subject.

"Not very *gut*." Lily said softly. "He was up all night coughing. *Maemm* is taking him to see a doctor today."

They shared a concern look thinking of their *daed*. With the weather becoming harsher, and colder it wasn't uncommon to fall ill. Not when they were outside continually taking care of their horses and livestock. The only problem with their *daed* was that he never knew when to slow down. Years of working hard were embedded deeply within him. There wasn't a memory of Matilda's that didn't involve her *daed* working the fields out of their *haus* or sitting next to him on a plough, listening to the soothing tones of his jovial voice It was hard telling him to stop even when they pleaded for him to rest. The *mensleit* of their community were all equally stubborn and refused to rest. Samuel had been no different when he fell ill and continued to push himself.

Matilda's eyes flickered closed when the scenario of their *daed's* death played in her mind. The thought of not seeing her *daed's* smiling face dug a painful and bottomless hole in her heart. She didn't even want to imagine living without her parents.

The jingle of the front door opening distracted her from those thoughts. Matilda quickly wiped her hands dry on her apron and entered the front of the bakery. She stopped short when piercing blue eyes and honey blonde hair belonging to Olivia greeted her on the other side of the counter.

"Matilda, right?" Olivia asked.

Matilda approached the counter cautiously. Her last exchange with Olivia hadn't exactly been pleasant, but she remained polite nonetheless. She took in the tight red sweater with a low neckline and tattered jeans that were equally tight. Matilda briefly wondered how Olivia could breathe given how tight her English clothes were, but she forced a smile on her face.

"Yes, what can I help you with?"

Olivia drummed her nails on the counter top. She scrutinized Matilda and frowned. "I'm looking for my brother," she said eventually. "My husband and I are in town for a break, and we were supposed to meet him. I'd call, but it seems that he has turned off his cell phone."

"I have no idea where he is."

"Are you sure? He seemed to like hanging out here all the time. He even talked about you quite a bit."

"I—"

She really had no response to any of that. Olivia studied her reaction but waited patiently for a response.

"I'm sorry, Matilda said. "I really have no idea where he is. I haven't seen him since Sunday,"

"If you do see him," Olivia started, her tone implying that she would, "please tell Ryan that we are staying at the same hotel we stayed before the wedding. I'd like to see him before he disappears off the grid."

"Disappears?"

"You know what I mean. He's been wanting to join the Amish faith for a while, and now he's finally pursuing it."

Nothing gave away Olivia's emotions or thoughts. Her face remained impassive and her tone neutral. There was no doubt that Ryan and Olivia were related since they shared the same off-putting ability to keep their emotions guarded.

She continued, "You do know that Ryan really is joining your community right?"

"I honestly have no idea what Ryan is doing exactly. I didn't realize he was all that serious."

"You don't know that he's stepped down from the company he built by himself and sold his house to live out of a hotel room or that he shut his cell phone off and threw away his computer?"

The information slowly processed in Matilda's mind. For a minute, her heart failed to beat and she swayed. There was no doubt anymore. Ryan would be joining the Amish faith and her community. It would be impossible to hide from him now. He was leaving behind an English life-style and his sister—the only family he had left in the world. Her heart ached slightly staring at Olivia who had relied on him through their mother's death

Matilda cleared the dryness from her throat and bowed her head to avoid Olivia's penetrating stare. "I honestly didn't know. If he feels like this is the right thing to do then there's no convincing him."

"That would be my brother. He gets an idea in his head and there's no changing it." Olivia laughed and smoothed her hand through the long strands of her hair "Well, if you see him, please pass the message on. I'd like to see him before we go back home."

"I promise I will tell him."

Olivia nodded curtly before turning to walk out the bakery. Her high-heeled boots clinked against the floor and it made her hips sway slightly. The door opened before she could reach it.

"Thanks," Olivia said shortly to whoever kept the door open.

She directed one last look in Matilda's direction before disappearing out of view.

Eli appeared in the doorway with snowflakes covering the tops of his shoulders and hat. He brushed them off outside before stepping into the warm bakery. "It smells wonderful in here."

Matilda's remained focused on the window outside as Olivia slipped into the passenger seat of a black car. She shook out a couple of snowflakes from her hair and then closed the door.

"*Ja*," she said, returning her attention to Eli. "Would you like a ham and cheese sandwich for lunch this time?"

"That would be *wunderbar.*"

She made the sandwich on freshly baked slices of bread and handed it to Eli. He smiled appreciatively, but picked at the edges of the sandwich nervously.

"I have to ask you something, Matilda."

Matilda's hand paused in putting the cash in the till. She saw his troubled look and slowly closed the register drawer.

"What is it?"

"I've been hearing things around the community. Things about..—"

"About Ryan?" she, said, finishing his thought. "You aren't the first person to come up to me and ask about it."

"I'm sorry. It's not my business or anyone else's, for that matter. I just wanted to know if what everyone is saying is true."

"Like what?"

Eli chewed on his bottom lip for a moment. "That you and him well—"

If things weren't so complicated thanks to Ryan's unsettling appearance and her own confused feelings towards him she would've found Eli's nerves endearing. She considered waving away whatever Eli heard, but she owed him honesty after everything he had done for her and her *kinner*.

"I knew him from a while ago, during my rumspringa and that's about it. There isn't anything else. He's here because he wants to be closer to *Gott*. I know what is being said, that he's joining to somehow get closer to me, but I have little to do with any of it."

Eli remained quiet for a while, taking in her words. She saw the gradual relief come over him. but she remained uneasy. Moving on from Samuel and learning to let someone else in never was easy from the start. Even if Ryan joined the church and belonged to their community, she would still struggle to let herself love another.

How could she even love another *mann*? Not after the life Samuel had built for her and their *kinner*.

"That's *gut* to hear, ." Eli said. "I wasn't sure if what Martha told me was true. Seeing Ryan at church and how he seemed to talk to you. I just didn't know."

As Eli rubbed the back of his neck, Matilda sighed inwardly at Martha's name. They were never confrontational with one another and even friendly since their *kinner* got along so well; but sometimes she felt that Martha harbored a bit of jealousy for her relationship with Samuel. Martha had been more than a little upset when Samuel ended their courtship to be with Matilda when she returned from rumspringa. In the end, it didn't surprise her that Martha said something to Eli.

"We're just friends. He doesn't know anyone here yet."

"I imagine he won't be friendless for very long." Eli said dryly.

Matilda bit her lip to contain the smile that wanted to spread across her face. "You're probably right about that but we are just friends."

"I worried about his intentions towards you"

She waved a dismissive hand. "I haven't even given courting a second thought."

The second those words left her mouth she realized the mistake. Something sparked in Eli's eyes. "I pray you aren't serious about that.

Matilda bowed her head then to avoid his stare and began to pray for *Gott* to give her guidance. She had no idea how she would get herself out of this current mess she found herself in.

The steady trickle of snowfall coated the buildings and mountains in white. Matilda gazed out the window of the bakery with a small smile as her *kinner* tossed snowballs in the air in the field across from the bakery. After picking them up from the schoolhouse, she had relented and allowed them to play in the snow before helping out in the bakery. Their happy laughter melted away any cold that had settled in Matilda's bones.

She returned to wiping the display cases clean. Starting tomorrow the phone would be ringing nonstop with Englischers ordering pies for their Thanksgiving dinners that would happen in a few days. Matilda would need every ounce of help from Lily and Rosella since her *maemm* was now sick as well after catching her *daed's* cold. That left her in charge of the bakery during a busy time that only added to her stress.

The distant clatter in the kitchen told Matilda that Lily was fulfilling her duties of preparing for tomorrow by cleaning and organizing. In less than an hour they would take the snowy ride home with hot chocolate in mugs to keep their hands warm and nothing sounded more pleasant than that to Matilda. The front door opened behind her and a blast of cold air greeted the back of Matilda's legs. She turned, expecting it to be a customer or someone from their community.

"Hey," Ryan said, his trademark grin on his face. "You look like you've gotten over your cold. That's good news."

"*Ja.* You're in a cheery mood."

Ryan started across the bakery with confident strides. With each step he took, the harder Matilda's heart hammered. She quickly placed herself behind the counter to keep a good amount of distance between them.

"Well, I have cheery news."

It was hard to ignore Ryan's good mood. She had grown accustomed to his guarded expressions, but seeing his obvious joy over something softened her defenses.

"What's that?"

"I wanted to apologize first about my sister coming in here. I know that she probably drilled you a bit."

"She seemed to have the idea that I knew where you were last week."

"Yeah, sorry. My sister isn't exactly supportive about me joining, and I had told her about us."

"Us?" Matilda echoed. She gave a dismaying shake of her head. "Ryan, there's no us. You—"

"I meant back when you were on rumspringa. I told her about you and what happened back then to our relationship."

She felt the sudden heat in her cheeks when Ryan raised his eyes from where they had been studying the display case with interest. Since his arrival to their community, not once had they mentioned the events during rumspringa and she wanted to keep it that way. She didn't need the community talking discussing her wicked behavior while on rumspringa. She could only imagine what the reactions would be.

"Before you tell me your news, I have to ask you something. A favor, to be specific."

She twisted her hands nervously in front of her. After straining to check the back kitchen, Matilda leaned across the counter so she could talk softly. "Please, don't mention to the Bishop or to anyone else what happened over rumspringa. I'd prefer to keep that between us."

"Who said anything about rumspringa? Lucy?

"I moved here to Monte Vista with my husband and family. Lucy stayed behind in Lancaster. Just please don't say anything. There's only two people who know and that's all."

"Is it really that big of a deal?" Ryan asked, staring at her with a mixture of amusement and bafflement.

Matilda scolded herself for piquing his curiosity and tried to come up with an answer.

"No, but things are different now. I just don't want everyone talking about it, that's all."

"Because they were such wicked things right, Mattie?" His smile turned into a sly grin.

Matilda cleared her throat in embarrassment and fanned herself with a dust rag to combat the sudden heat in her face. "Don't do that." She admonished breathlessly. "If you are going to join the church, you can't say things like that."

"Sorry. It was just too easy. I don't understand why you're concerned. You're the one who said what you did on rumspringa wouldn't get you into trouble with the church."

"That is true. I don't gossip going around the community about me. I have my *kinner* to worry about, and—" My parents would be disappointed if they heard and it would only confirm my *maemm's* thoughts about you.

He clasped her shoulder and she twitched at the touch. He gave her an assuring smile. "I won't say anything. I promise."

She relaxed at his words and instinctively reached for his hand. That one simple touch kindled a fire within her heart.

The front door opened with a bang. A snowy air carried the moment away as Matilda hurriedly moved away. They both turned and saw Eli struggling to the shut door against the howling wind.

"Here, let me help you." Ryan said.

He left the front counter and helped Eli push the door closed. Matilda looked out the window and sw her *kinner* still playing in the snow, oblivious to the strong winds.

"*Danka*," Eli said curtly.

He looked at Matilda standing behind the counter and at Ryan. and kept whatever comments he had quiet. In that second Matilda was grateful for their Amish roots. Eli would never confront someone or create a scene even if he were upset.

"Matilda, I need your help," he said, ignoring Ryan completely now. "Betty has caught a cold, and she needs you. I've tried giving her teas, but I think she's in need of a *maemm's* touch."

"Of course," Matilda said.. "Let me close the bakery up and I will come with you."

All traces of her conversation with Ryan faded away as her motherly instincts kicked in. After rushing Lily out of the kitchen and locking the bakery up, Matilda turned to tell Ryan goodbye as she walked out into the snowy afternoon. Ryan trailed after her. She made sure that her *kinner* and Lily hitched up Pepper without any difficulties before addressing Ryan.

They stood in the middle of the parking lot with Eli sitting in his buggy. He waited for Matilda, leather reigns gathered in his hands as he watched them.

"I'm sorry, but I must go, she said and gave his forearm a quick squeeze.

She turned to go, but he held her back. It took all her control not to reach up and wipe away the snowflakes that had fallen onto his head.

"Are you sure you don't need a ride there?" Ryan asked again. He flourished the keys in the air. "I honestly have no problems giving you a ride if it's that serious."

"Ach, that's okay. We—"

"That's all right, Ryan." Eli interrupted. He had steered the buggy alongside Matilda. "Our transportation is by buggy. We can get there as fast as a car."

Matilda slipped out of Ryan's grasp. She offered him one last apologetic smile and climbed to the passenger side of the buggy. Eli flicked the reigns without waiting for her to settle in and wrap a blanket around their legs.

As they trotted away at a quick pace Matilda turned around to find the parking lot already empty. She felt a twinge of disappointment when she realized that Ryan hadn't told her the news.

CHAPTER TEN

Whatever news Ryan wanted to tell her never came. Thanksgiving passed in a busy blur for Matilda baking pies with the help of Rosella and Lily while her *maemm* recovered from her bout of illness. Disappointment faded to uncertainty as Thanksgiving and Christmas passed with no sign of Ryan.

"Still no sign of him?" Lily asked.

Matilda wrapped another pie in cellophane and set in the counter. "*Nee*. Not a word."

"I wonder what happened." Lily said, frowning deeply. "It doesn't seem like him to just not say anything."

"I have no idea, Lily. He must've decided that joining wasn't the right thing."

She managed to keep her face collected to hide the tumultuous emotions inside, as she busied herself in the task of getting pies ready for pick-up. She didn't want to think about the small bit of hope that had developed over the past few weeks. She also didn't want to think about the hurt she felt at the thought that Ryan didn't confide in her about his doubts in joining.

It was bound to happen. Devoting oneself to *Gott* wasn't easy and nor was their way of living.

"It's better this way, too," Matilda spoke out loud, turning to face Lily with a sad smile. "It would've been too much for him trying to live here. Not with everyone talking the way they are about him."

"You mean how people are talking about you and him."

"*Nee.* That's not it. I—"

"Honestly, *sveeshtah*," Lily cut in, shaking her head in exasperation, "How much longer are you going to deny this? It's obvious to the entire community."

Her heart stopped beating for several seconds. The world slowed down as her sister's casual statement processed through her brain. Matilda turned around shakily to look at Lily with trepidation.

"What's obvious to the community?"

Lily rolled her eyes. "No need to look all dramatic, Matilda. It's honestly not a big deal that everyone can tell that you two have had feelings for one another or maybe currently do.."

A hiss of air escaped through Matilda's clenched teeth in relief. Her secret was still a secret and that's all she cared about. The dread stemmed from the community knowing that something had happened between the two of them.

Maybe it would be better if Ryan left in search of *Goll* with a different community. In only a few short weeks he turned everything upside down and exposed a part of her past that she felt uncomfortable making visible.

"It doesn't matter now, she said. He's not around anymore."

Matilda gathered the pies in her arms and left the kitchen before Lily could say anything else. She nudged the display case door open with her knee and placed them inside neatly.

"So, you're admitting it then?"

The door swooshed open behind her as Lily followed her out. Matilda closed the display case and picked up a dust rag.

"*Maemm* says we need to dust. I'll start with the—"

Lily snatched the rag promptly from Matilda's hands and tossed it carelessly back on the counter.

"Have you ever thought that maybe why you feel the way you do is because you haven't let go of Samuel?"

"I don't want to talk about this, Lily. Let it be."

"*Nee*. You're my sister, and I love you. What are you so afraid of?"

I can't believe my almost sixteen-year old sister is interrogating me." A dry amusement at the thought, nearly made her smile. She smoothed a hand over her face and leaned back against the counter. "Things are complicated. You wouldn't understand what's going on even if I told you."

Lily squared her shoulders, and crossed her arms determinedly across her chest. Her arched and challenging brow that echoed their *maemm's*.

"Try me."

Matilda debated on walking away. How could her sister even begin to understand what her heart was going through? She took in her sister's smooth and pale cheeks dusted with freckles. She was all innocent and light, not darkened with any past hurts or grievances. Soon, she would be venturing out into the world as Matilda had done so many years ago.

She would discover that not everything, including love, was black or white. There were tons of confusing grey between.

Matilda's heart ached thinking of Lily, who's always so gentle and compassionate, coming across hardships that could break her kind-hearted nature.

"A new part of your life will begin and it's going to be exciting. It was for me too back when I was your age, but things won't be so simple. *Jah*, I had feelings for Ryan back then' iIntense ones that I still feel today, but it would never work. Not then, not now.

"Why wouldn't it work now? If you still have feelings for him."

"Because I also still love Samuel. He was my *mann*, Lily. That's not a simple commitment that I can throw away just because of old feelings. I have my *kinner* to think about too. Samuel was their *daed* and will always be. How do you think they will feel if I married someone else?"

"I think they'd grow to understand that you can't do everything by yourself. I understand that Samuel was your *mann*, but I think it's more than that. You're afraid of falling in love with Ryan again. I think you're even afraid of falling in love with Eli."

"Wouldn't you be after losing someone?"

"*Jah*, of course, but I get the feeling that you're hiding something. Even *maemm* has commented on it and all of it circles around Ryan."

"I'm not hiding anything, Lily." Tears clouded Matilda's vision. She turned away from Lily's prodding eyes and grabbed the abandoned dust rag.

"I don't want to talk about this anymore. We need to get back to work."

"But—"

The front door opened, and a blast of December air swept through the bakery. Eli emerged through the door brushing off snow from the thick wool coat he wore. He scuffed his boots on the welcome mat to free them of any gravel and mud. Matilda chewed on her bottom lip to keep the sigh of disappointment inside. She still held hope that Ryan would walk through the bakery door with the grin she had always loved.

"Good morning," Eli said, smiling warmly at them both. "Could I bother one of you for a sandwich before I go to work?"

"I have to pull out some pies from the oven," Lily said.

She disappeared through the door before Matilda could excuse herself. Matilda slowly set the dust rag back on the counter. Unable to meet Eli's gaze, she lowered them down to the loaves of freshly baked bread.

"What type of sandwich would you like?"

"Perhaps a warm turkey sandwich would be *gut* for the road?"

"*Ja.* That will keep you warm on your way to work."

An awkward silence descended on the bakery. Matilda kept her back turned to Eli as she prepared his sandwich. The soft hair on the back of her neck stood on edge as the sensation of being watched intently filled her. When she turned back, Eli looked away.

"Here," she said. and slid the carefully wrapped sandwich across the counter.

He picked it up with a grateful smile, but his eyes remained on hers curiously. "Are you all right, Matilda? You seem a bit down about something."

Honey blonde hair passing the window caught Matilda's eyes before she could reply. Her heart stalled briefly in hope as the front door opened, but Rosella emerged from the waves of snow crashing down upon the valley. Strands of hair that escaped from beneath Rosella's prayer *kapp* were damp from the snow and pasted themselves to the side of her neck. She also brushed away the snowflakes from wool coat and slipped off her gloves. Her winter boots squeaked on the linoleum floor and wet footprints trailed after her. When Isaac and Matthew didn't appear in the bakery, Matilda sighed in exasperation.

"Where are your *bruders*?" Matilda asked. "They better not be outside playing in the snow. Isaac has a cold."

Rosella shrugged her shoulders indifferently. "They started a snowball fight when we left the schoolhouse, and it didn't stop on the way up here."

That explained the pink tinge to Rosella's right cheek and her damp strands of hair.

"I'm hungry, *maemm*. Can I have a slice of whoopie pie?"

Rosella pointed at the whoopie pie sitting on the counter, waiting for Ryan to pick up.

"*Nee*, Rosella." Matilda said, shaking her head. "Not until after dinner and that is in another five hours. Go get your *bruders* for me."

"I can get them before I go to work," Eli spoke up, setting the sandwich back down on the counter. "I understand how a snowball fight works."

He smiled fleetingly at Matilda before exiting the bakery. Rosella turned to look at Matilda. "He can't have a snowball fight with us. That was our thing with *daed*."

Matilda laid a consoling hand on Rosella's arm. "I know that, Rosella. He isn't trying to replace your *daed*."

"Well, sometimes I think he is." She mumbled under her breath.

Her *kinner* would never accept another *daed*. The pit of Matilda's stomach dropped slightly at the realization, but she expected it. Samuel had been a kind *daed* that loved them dearly, and it would be hard for any man to not live in that shadow.

The conversation with Lily repeated in her mind again. "I just get this feeling that you're hiding something." She studied Rosella carefully, taking in the delicate bone structure of her slender face and the unconscious way her eyes darted to every sound. In so many ways Rosella was like Ryan, from their matching eyes and hair, to the confident air around them and their similar mannerisms. It wouldn't take long for anyone to figure it out. What would she do then? Pray that *Gott* would help her weather the harsh seas that would surely follow. She couldn't lie about it. Not when Matthew and Isaac shared the same traits as Samuel's from their boyish grins and innocent playfulness. They acted differently from Rosella whose sense of humor was much like Ryan's, sly and quick-witted. Still, Samuel was Rosella's *daed* all the same, the first one to hold her after she was born and to kiss bruised knees.

"No one will replace your *daed*, Rosella," Matilda said, quietly

Rosella met Matilda's gaze. Rosella kept her emotions carefully guarded. Another uncanny ability that she shared with Ryan.

"You're right. No one can and will ever replace *daed*."

The ride to the King's *haus* was filled with the dull crunch of snow underneath the buggy wheels. Fields were covered thoroughly with thick blankets of white and the evergreen tree branches drooped from the weight. The steady stream of snowfall shielded the mountains from sight, but every so often Matilda occasionally caught sight of the outlines of the mountains.

Matilda raised her eyes upwards to the twisting clouds above. She squinted against the blinding white and the wetness clouding her vision, but rejoiced in the feeling of the soft snowflakes caressing her face. A muffled silence filled the valley as it always did whenever there was a heavy snowfall. She loved the purity of winter, and how clean it was.

The shift of the blanket across her lap brought Matilda's attention back to her *kinner* huddled in the buggy alongside her. Steam curled from the mugs of hot chocolate they clasped tightly in their hands to keep themselves warm. They were unusually quiet this morning, staring out at their surroundings with unseeing eyes.

She wished she could read their minds sometimes.

They reached the King *haus* a few minutes before church would start. Matilda unbuckled Pepper from the buggy and lead him into an unoccupied stall in the barn. She slipped off her wool gloves, tucking them in the pocket of her dress and started through the barn doors to collide with something warm and solid.

"Oof."

Matilda took a hasty step back from the sturdy chest she had collided with and flushed with embarrassment at who it was.

"I'm sorry, Eli. I wasn't paying attention to where I was going."

He rubbed the spot where Matilda's chin had collided with his sternum, but amusement belied his eyes.

"I noticed. Hold on, I'll walk with you to the *haus*. I need to talk to you anyway."

Snow touched the bottom of her dress. Matilda hitched the wet cotton fabric of her dress skirts up ever so slightly as they trudged through the snow towards the *haus* where the rest of their community gathered. Smoke billowed out from the stone chimney on the roof top and disappeared in the surrounding whiteness. Matilda's pace quickened at the thought of sitting in a warm living room and singing hymns.

They reached the front porch steps and kicked the snow from their boots. Matilda brushed off the snowflakes from her shoulders and reached up to dry her face, but calloused finger tips beat her to it. She jerked in surprise at the contact as Eli's thumb wiped away a trail of wetness from her jaw line and took a hasty step backwards from him.

Hurt flashed in Eli's eyes when she drew back, but his face soon colored in shame behind the coarseness of his beard. He had touched her openly with members of their community inside and with a bit of boldness that surprised them both.

Matilda's breath puffed out in front of her in a white moist cloud. She felt the center of her own cheeks flame with embarrassment.

"I'm sorry, Matilda. I don't know what got into me." he said.

"I think—," she paused to catch her breath and still the jitteriness within. "I think it's best if we took a bit of a step back from one another. For a little while."

"Is that really what you want?"

He didn't bother hiding the disappointment on his face. Matilda cast her eyes downward guiltily and studied their wet boots before she spoke.

"I honestly don't know what I want right now, Eli. It's just so hard to move on to someone else after Samuel died" she whispered, bowing her head even further.

"Perhaps if you try to—"

"Please, don't try to persuade me," Matilda interrupted before he could go on any further. She raised her tear-filled eyes up to Eli's. "My *kinner*, they aren't ready to have another *daed* figure in their lives. I'm not even sure if they ever will be willing to accept anyone new in their lives."

"I understand that your *kinner* are still grieving for their *daed*. My *kinner* grieve for their *maemm*, but I can't do both jobs. They'll have to understand someday that you can't do everything on your own," Eli said gently.

"I will if that's what it takes to keep them happy." Eli tilted his head to the side ever so slightly and looked at her through skeptical eyes.

"Are you sure this isn't about the Englischer Ryan?"

"*Nee!*" Matilda insisted. "It has nothing to do with him. I—"

"Then give us a chance to work. I care about you, Matilda. I could grow to love you if you can allow yourself to love me. Think about how much easier it would be to have a *mann* again to take care of you and the *kinner*."

Matilda's eyes drifted close. She had imagined letting Eli into their lives several times and she didn't want to give Eli any false hope for them to work if it didn't feel right deep down. Before accepting Samuel's marriage proposal, she had prayed long and hard to *Gott*. She knew it had been the right decision at the time when Samuel placed a hand over her stomach and smiled happily. He had fit into her life seamlessly without a hitch.

"I'm not sure if I can even fall in love again, Eli. I care about you too, but I don't want to give you any false hope," Matilda said quietly.

She opened her eyes to find Eli's looking off in the distance. They stood on the porch with the snow continuing to fall down around them and shivered at the coldness that clung to the morning. The smell of crisp evergreen pine and smoke from the fire inside filled Matilda's lungs when she breathed in.

"I'm sorry, Matilda," Eli said, breaking the silence with his deep voice. "I just think you're a wonderful *maemm* and a beautiful woman. Any man would be lucky to have you as a *fraa*. Samuel was lucky."

Matilda smiled tremulously. She tenderly reached up to cup Eli's cheek, coarse beard hairs tickling her palm.

"You'll find someone again and she'll be a lucky *fraa* when that day comes. *Gott* has a plan for each of us."

Eli's lips twitched with a ghost of a smile, but hurt still lingered openly.

"*Jah*. He does." He reached up to squeeze Matilda's hand briefly before letting it drop. "We better go inside. Church is about to start."

"I'll be there in a minute."

He nodded and then opened the front door. Warm conversation and air briefly touched Matilda before the door shut firmly behind Eli. She let out a shaky breath and leaned up against the wooden railing, placing a hand above her frantically beating heart.

"Tell me that was the right decision, *Gott*. Tell me I made the right decision," Matilda whispered.

The sound of horse hooves swishing through the snow and wheels groaning drew Matilda's eyes to the road. A lone buggy trotted forward steadily down the driveway and to the barn. She squinted, trying to discern the two figures huddled together. The swirling snow made it hard to see.

Once the buggy crossed in front of the *haus*, Matilda recognized the Bishop's older brother, John, huddled on the passenger side. Something kept her rooted to the spot as the driver of the buggy jumped out lithely and walked around the buggy to help John step down.

John spotted her standing on the front porch and waved an age spotted hand in a friendly greeting.

"Good morning, Matilda! Quite the snowfall we are getting, eh?"

Matilda smiled down at him as the older man trudged his way through the shin-high snow.

"Good morning to you, John. *Jah*, quite the snowfall."

She reached down a helpful hand to help him up the wet porch stairs. The smell of tobacco and *kaffee* clung to John's wool coat.

"I'm told it will be good for our crops, to have all this snow." John said, waving a hand at the land around them. "I don't know about you, dear, but being old doesn't mix well with the cold. I say we could do without all this snow."

"I agree," Matilda replied, smiling. "Let me walk you inside."

John batted her hand away. "No need. I may be old, but I can still get around just fine."

He opened the door and slipped inside, closing the door without waiting for her. Voices, singing in unison, reached her ears. She palmed her eyes dry and went to open the door when a voice called out.

"Mattie."

Her stomach flopped almost painfully at the sound of the familiar syrupy folds of Ryan's voice. She blinked rapidly for a few seconds, trying to discern if it were her imagination that heard Ryan or that it really was him.

Her hand slipped from the cold doorknob and hung loosely by her side. With a deep breath, she slowly turned around expecting to find nothing but snow and wind. Instead, a tall figure stood on the bottom porch step, dressed in black trousers and a thick wool coat. The honey-colored hair and sapphire eyes were unmistakable.

The world teeter tottered dangerously beneath Matilda's feet. She stared down at Ryan in shock, completely speechless for a moment. The sound of the minister's voice, muffled from being inside, filled the silence stretching between them. All Matilda could think was, "You're here. You're actually here."

Ryan arched an eyebrow and stretched out his arms, studying them with mock surprise. "Why, yes. I'm actually here and not elsewhere. Thank you for that assurance."

She ignored his sarcastic reply. "How-how-I thought you were gone. I haven't seen you since before Thanksgiving."

"I know. I told my sister that I would spend the holidays with her one last time before coming here. So, that's where I've been."

"Ach."

Ryan climbed the rest of the porch steps. He towered over her easily, having to tilt his head down so their eyes could connect. The smell of freshly washed linens and soap filled Matilda's nose when she breathed him in discreetly.

"Did you doubt that I would go through with this?" He asked, playfulness threading his voice.

"Maybe," Matilda admitted softly. "I wouldn't be truthful if I said that I had no doubts about you being here."

They stood toe to toe with a few inches of space between them. An invisible rope tightened around Matilda's waist and tugged her closer. Their fingers barely brushed one another's.

"Let me erase those doubts then. The church is giving me one year to live here as a test. John has been gracious enough to let me live with him. In return, I will help him around the farm since his age is catching up with him. If all goes well, then I can be baptized and be a part of the community."

Matilda tried to take a step back, but her legs refused to move. A haziness filled her mind and made it difficult to concentrate. She struggled to breathe properly at Ryan's proximity

"You shouldn't be joining just because of me. Join because of *Gott*."

"I am joining because of *Gott*. We already established that my motives are to join because of *Gott*. You just happen to be a bonus."

He brushed a knuckle along her cheek, and smiled softly down at her. Matilda jolted at the contact, and to her horror, felt herself leaning in towards the touch. The same touch that caused her to scold Eli. She drew back promptly and put some space between them.

"You can't just come in here and think that we can pick up on things. There are rules, different from the ones you are used too."

"I can learn them. I'm a fast learner."

"I have my *kinner* to think of too, Ryan. They lost their *daed*, and I don't even know if—"

Ryan shushed her with a finger on her lips. She felt her eyes widen at the rather intimate contact and opened her mouth to scold him, but was rendered mute by the cloud of Ryan's breath hitting her face.

"I understand that, Mattie. Trust me when I say that I do understand. I don't know why are you so afraid of me being here, but there's nothing you can do about it. I'm here to stay, and you can either like it or hate it. It's really up to you."

Her eyes drifted closed. The past few weeks of building up walls and guarding herself from the emotions Ryan stirred within her crumbled. He was right. There was nothing she could but pray that everything would be fine in the end.

Even if Ryan discovered the truth.

"I do hope that you won't hate me being here. I could really use your help throughout this whole process," Ryan whispered.

Matilda blew out a defeated sigh. She gently pushed away Ryan's finger from her lips and then tentatively laced her fingers through his chilled fingers.

"I suppose I have no other choice now, do I?"

"No. Not really."

They laughed quietly together. Ryan's fingers slipped from hers, and he reached out to open the door, holding it open for her. Warm air rushed out from the narrow hallway and the sound of their community singing songs of praise. Matilda felt a smile spread across her face and something eased up from deep in her.

"Shall we?" Ryan asked, extending out a hand to her.

Gott truly had a plan for her. For the first time since Samuel's death, she could see His fingers sewing the threads of her life back together. This was her purpose, to help Ryan along his journey and she thanked *Gott* for the honor of helping Ryan along his spiritual path.

Matilda didn't hesitate to grab his hand as she passed by him. They shared a brief smile before entering the narrow hallway to join the chorus of voices singing hymns of praise.

"Yes, we shall."

She turned to glance back at Ryan one last time, reluctantly wondering if there was more to *Gott's* calling. For now, she decided, the answer to that question didn't matter. A year's worth of time stretched on before them.

A lot could happen within a year.

Yes, the story of Matilda and Ryan continues in book #3, AN AMISH TEST. It's a year of testing for Ryan and a trial for Mattie. Will their love survive and will Ryan finally become fully Amish?

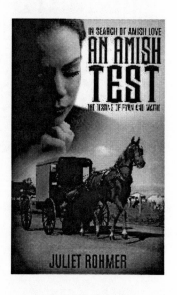

AN AMISH TEST
www.AmishChristianRomance.com
Curious to learn more about Mattie's Rumspringa and how it ended? Read the short story BEYOND GOODBYE.

BEFORE GOODBYE
www.AmishChristianRomance.com

When young Matilda Beachey is talked into going on rumspringa with her best friend, she has no plans other than to return home to her Amish life as soon as possible. Instead she goes from Matilda to Mattie and meets Ryan Meyers, an attractive, sexy older boy who teaches her a lot more than the *Englischers* way of life. What will she do when it's time to return home to her life and the best friend who patiently waits for her return?

EXCERPT: *AN AMISH TEST*

The Testing of Mattie and Ryan

March crashed down upon the San Luis Valley like a rogue wave of unusually warm air. Hopeful buds appeared on bare tree branches, and tender vegetation stirred to life. Columbines sprouted upwards from the damp earth, their vibrant colors peeking out cautiously in the direction of the sun.

Matilda King wiped a hand along the smooth plane of her forehead. She squinted against the bright sunlight from where she stood on the front porch and looked in the direction of the Sangre De Cristo Mountain range. Snow still clung to the mountain sides and even in the fields directly below them. She took a brief moment from cleaning the *haus* of dirt and dust to pray to *Gott* that the warm weather would continue, but she couldn't shake that feeling of dread that blossomed in the center of her chest.

Warm weather in early spring promised two things: chilly temperatures that returned in April and lasted to the beginning of June, or a drought. Matilda prayed that neither occurred. Five springs ago, she remembered vividly how Samuel had spent the night covering the garden with potato sacks but the late snow in early June had won. They replanted and prayed for a warm fall. That summer had been short, dry, and cooler than normal. She'd never forget the distressed look on Samuel's face as he took in the small piles of their harvest, but it didn't last.

Her Samuel always had a backup plan. He traded several hours of fixing buggies for more vegetables and used the Farmers Market to purchase meat to supply them through the harsh winter.

Matilda felt her stomach tighten in longing. She would give anything to have Samuel and his backup plans once again, especially now that she could be facing yet another hard planting season.

"*Ach!*"

The sound of Isaac's voice crying in surprise drew Matilda's attention back to where her *kinner* were currently taking advantage of the strange heat at the beginning of March. She assessed the situation and smiled.

"Mama!" Isaac cried, pointing a pale finger at Rosella. "She sprayed water at me."

A large wet stain covered the front of Isaac's button shirt. Rosella blinked innocently with the hose on the muddy ground alongside her. "I didn't do anything. Isaac got himself wet."

"I did not!" He glared at Rosella. "You sprayed me with water. Now, my shirt is all wet."

"Don't be such a *bobli.*"

Matilda stepped off the front porch to intervene before a fight could ensue. Her *kinner* loved one another, but being cooped up all winter in the *haus* had worn on everyone's nerves. She approached Isaac and placed a gentle hand on his head and felt the heat of the sun in the silky strands of hair.

"Go inside and change. I don't want you to catch a cold while working in a damp shirt."

"But it's warm out," he protested, now happy to forget his wet shirt.

"Inside, now."

At the firmness of her tone, Isaac's shoulders dropped. He shot Rosella one last glowering glare before disappearing into the *haus*. Meanwhile, Matthew looked first at Matilda, then at Rosella. Matilda tried not to smile when Mathew, clearly sensing the tension building between Rosella and his mother, grabbed a watering pail and beat a hasty retreat to the garden.

Rosella stared at the ground in an obvious attempt to avoid her mother's gaze. Over the past few months, Matilda had noticed a change in Rosella's behavior. While normally well-behaved (besides occasional bouts of sassiness), her daughter's mood seemed to have darkened. Rosella often withdrew into silent thoughts and replied to her mother's inquires in a strained voice. Her *bruders* seemed to be the main target of her changing moods, and Matilda wondered what sort of confrontation was going on between them.

Rosella was the first to speak. "Aren't you going to say something?" she asked, her voice flat and surly.

"I was hoping you would tell me what was going on," Matilda replied and leveled a pointed glance at her when Rosella looked up. "Particularly, what's going on with you?"

Those all too familiar sapphire eyes shifted away, veiling whatever turbulent emotions were at play within her daughter. Matilda sighed. It was a subtle withdrawal. She had always been close to Rosella, but she knew eventually her daughter would exhibit some of this behavior. Rosella might be Amish through and through, but she had also reached her teenage years.

Matilda took a deep breath and tried a different approach. She took a step towards Rosella, while offering a smile of peace. "Whatever it is, Rosella, you can tell me. I promise not to get mad if that is what worries you."

"That isn't what I worry about."

Another wall. A headache started to pound in the back of Matilda's head. She refused to show any sign of inward aggravation at her daughter's distant behavior.

"Well?" she said, when Rosella didn't continue. "What's going on?"

Rosella twisted her hands in the apron tied tightly around her trim waist as she chewed on her bottom lip. Matilda remained quiet as she met her daughter's searching look. A warm breeze played with an errant strand of honey blonde hair that escaped the pins of her daughter's *kapp*.

"You promise to not get mad or defensive over it?"

"*Ja*," Matilda said, agreeing quickly and happy to see a break in the wall, "I promise. Whatever it is, I promise to be open."

"Okay. I—"

The distant crunch of horse hooves on gravel alerted both of them that someone was coming down their road. Matilda noticed how Rosella glanced over her shoulder and tensed when she caught sight of the driver sitting in the buggy seat.

"I'm going inside," she muttered, kicking the hose out of the way. "I'm not feeling *gut*."

'Rosella—"

Her oldest gave no indication of hearing her plea. Instead, Rosella stomped up the front porch steps and slammed the door behind her. Matilda felt the pounding headache spread and rubbed her temples with the pads of her fingers as she turned to look up at the driver of the buggy.

Golden strands of hair sparkled in the warm sunlight and appeared to glow with more brightness than usual. Matilda couldn't stop herself as she took in the chiseled facial features and the strong hands grasping the leather reigns in such a sure way. Dressed in traditional Amish clothes, Ryan Myers remained unbearably handsome to look upon from his strong physique to his clean-shaven jaw; a sign of his marriage status.

"Morning," he said, flashing a grin that showed off his white teeth. "I was just taking this buggy for a spin to check out my work."

"So you came by my *haus*?" she said dryly.

Her strained question seemed to dampen his cheerful mood. He would be in a *gut* mood Matilda thought with a small inward smile. Adjusting to the Amish way of life had not been exactly easy for Ryan since the start of his testing period in January. The harsh winter elements didn't help him much when he had to chop wood outside in the middle of a frigid night or learn how to keep a fire going all night in the wood stove.

"How do you people live without electricity?" Ryan complained one afternoon, nursing a cold and a bad mood with a cup of chamomile tea. "I mean, the wood stove is great and all, but having to put wood in the thing every two hours is disrupting my sleep schedule. I might as well have a newborn baby if this is how it will be."

"I'll show you how to keep a fire going all night," Matilda volunteered, hoping to assure him. If *Gott* wanted her to help him along with his journey, she could surely show him the trick Samuel had shown her when it came to keeping the house warm at night.

She tried to keep her distance, though, and only offered help when needed. They were, after all, just friends. The statement felt irritatingly overused by now from how frequently Matilda repeated it to neighbors, friends, and even to her family. Ryan naturally glued himself to Matilda since joining the community for his testing period, and it was a bit unnerving sometimes to know that he trusted her that much. He had taken up a job in the same buggy shop Samuel used to work in and lived with their Bishop's older *bruder* who needed the help around the farm and *haus*. Ryan made it a point to stop by the bakery every lunch break to talk with Matilda, and to run through the Pennsylvania Dutch she was teaching him.

"I'm sorry?" Ryan posed it as a question, but a confused frown settled in his brow. "Did I break some sort of rule again by coming by the house? I seem to do that a lot more frequently now."

Matilda bit her tongue to keep her thoughts to herself. The first few months had been fine what with Ryan getting used to putting aside the luxuries of an English lifestyle. He seemed to be more at peace than when he first arrived in their community. Although he was willing and eager to learn every aspect of their lifestyle, Matilda's skepticism still continued to grow every day. She caught his confused frowns at church as he tried to understand the fast flowing sermons and saw a sadness that sometimes occupied his eyes when no one was watching.

Tiny breaks splintered Ryan's magnetic personality, but apparently she was the only one who noticed. The rest of the community was either smitten by his charming tongue on the rare occasions when he would talk, or they had their doubts that someone like him could truly live for *Gott*.

Matilda was also not unaware of the undercurrent of tension that pulled at them since what had been said back in January when Ryan first embraced their lifestyle and embarked on this year of testing. She truly believed *Gott* had a plan for both of them and Ryan insisted that he felt the same way. She prayed every day, seeking *Gott's* advice, and searching for answers on the direction of their relationship. Sure, there were the flirtatious comments that slipped from Ryan's tongue that had Matilda's blood quickening, but she was quick to calm herself and refrain from temptation through prayer and her strength in *Gott*. She knew any growing attachment toward Ryan would allow those old feelings to be stirred and would put her directly on the path for trouble.

Matilda wiped her sweaty palms on the front of her apron and absently smoothed a few wrinkles from her blue dress before answering Ryan's question. She still felt a bit odd wearing colors even though the period of wearing mourning clothes had finally ended. For her, the change was only on the physical level. Within her heart she still missed and mourned Samuel.

"You can't just show up to my *haus*." she said, trying to keep the exasperation out of her voice. "I have my *kinner* here, and I already have to keep explaining to the community that we are just friends. It does not look *gut* when you show up without a reason."

The rebuke went either unnoticed or Ryan was simply unperturbed by the rumors swirling around. He glanced over at the nearest neighboring farm, and then looked back at Matilda with a scoff.

"There's no one around to talk about us." he said. "Why do you listen to all that talk anyway? I don't listen or give a second thought to how the community thinks I won't even make it."

Ryan dropped the reigns and stretched his long arms above him. The casual gesture made Matilda squirm. She kept one eye trained to look out for her *kinner* who were already confused as to why Ryan made frequent visits. Her *kinner* seemed wary of him and his intentions, as was she.

"Is there something that you need, Ryan? I have a lot to do around the *haus*."

"You're doing work on a Saturday? It's the weekend."

"You have been here for how many months, Ryan? You know that we work on Saturdays and rest on Sundays."

Ryan shrugged and gave her one of his expansive smiles. "I still propose that everyone should have the weekend off. Maybe I'll suggest it to the Bishop tomorrow morning."

Matilda tried to keep a lid on her irritation as it bubbled dangerously over. Little comments like those that he uttered more frequently lately only added to her doubts about Ryan's commitment to *Gott* and the *Ordnung*. All the more reason to put distance between them.

When she didn't respond, Ryan held up his hands in surrender. "Only kidding, Mattie," he said, "I was just making a joke."

"Don't call me—"

"Mattie. I got it," he said, gathering the reins again and keeping a cool expression. "I'll let you be so you can stay in a grumpy mood."

Matilda stared up at him, trying to read his emotions. He met her gaze evenly before flicking the reigns gently and with a cluck of his tongue, gracefully turning the buggy around to head back up the road.

Just like that he left her standing on the front lawn of her *haus*, his antics leaving her torn between irritation and amusement. She glanced over her shoulder towards the garden, but found Matthew patting the ground to assess how much water the garden needed. The flutter of curtains upstairs drew her attention and for the briefest second she caught Rosella standing at the window, staring with yet one more scowl toward the vanishing horse and buggy.

It clicked then as to the source of Rosella's moods, and deep down Matilda felt the flutter of fear take flight once again. "*Gott* help me," she said, praying out loud.

AN AMISH TEST

Visit Juliet Rohmer's Amazon author page and FOLLOW.

See all her books.

ALSO BY JULIET ROHMER

A MAIL ORDER BRIDE HISTORICAL ROMANCE

COMING IN 2016: CIVIL WAR BRIDES

Love Amish fiction? Then you will probably find stories about young women who, after the Civil War, found themselves in all sorts of life situations where finding a husband became almost impossible. Discover how they handled this new era and whether they found true love in their midst.

For more information, go to
www.AmishChristianRomance.com

THE RECIPE

A Good Amish Whoopie Pie
Bake 350° 10-12 minutes — Yield: 2 dozen

1/2 cup water
1.2 cup baking cocoa
1 - 1/2 cup sugar
1/2 cup shortening
2 eggs
1/2 cup buttermilk
1 tsp vanilla extract
1 tsp baking powder
1/4 tsp salt
1 tsp baking soda
2 - 2/3 cups flour, all-purpose

Combine the baking cocoa and water in a small bowl. Let sit and cool for five (5) minutes.

Using a large bowl, cream both the shortening and the sugar until the mixture is light and fluffy. Add vanilla, eggs, and the cocoa mixture.

Mix the rest of the dry ingredients (flour, baking powder, salt, and baking soda) and slowly alternate adding to the creamy mixture with the buttermilk. Beat well each time.

Using a tablespoon, drop the mixture onto a greased baking sheet about two (2) inches apart. Take the back of the spoon and flatten slightly.

Bake for 10-12 minutes at 350° until firm. Place on wire racks to cool

The Whoopie Pie Creamy Filling

3 tbsp flour, all-purpose
salt, a dash
1 cup milk (2%)
1 1/2 cup sugar, confectioners'
3/4 cup shortening
2 tsp vanilla extract

Combine the all-purpose flour with the salt in a small saucepan. Whisk in the milk, gradually, until the mixture is smooth. Cook, stirring, over medium-high until thick (takes about 5-7 minutes). Remove from heat, cover, and refrigerate. Must be completely cool.

Using a small bowl, add the sugar, vanilla, and shortening and cream until it, too, is light and fluffy. Add the above milk mixture. Beat for 7 minutes until mixture is fluffy.

Spread the filling onto half of the cookies. Place the other half of the cookies on the top of the mixture.

Store in refrigerator.

ABOUT THE AUTHOR

Juliet Rohmer spends her days writing, reading, and researching. While she's not Amish, she formed a deep attachment for the Amish during her early years in Pennsylvania and values their deeply spiritual lifestyle. She enjoys writing inspirational stories whether they happen today or in years past. Fascinated with the Amish and with the post-Civil War era and the rise of mail order brides, Juliet looks forward to sharing their stories told in new and fresh ways.

For updates about new releases, as well as exclusive promotions, be sure and sign up for her VIP mailing list at AmishChristianRomance.com.

Follow Juliet Rohmer's Amazon Author page and like her Facebook page.

Amazon.com/Author/julietrohmer

Amish Romance Christian Inspirational Romance --
Juliet Rohmer

ENJOYED THIS BOOK?

You've made it to the end and I love it. Having a reader make it all the way through is a writer's dream for every story written. Enjoyed the story, please consider leaving an honest review. Reviews are a big help to all authors. They also let others know how much you enjoyed the story. You can leave your review on Amazon, or on Goodreads, LibraryThing or the sites wherever you bought the book. Your review means a great deal.

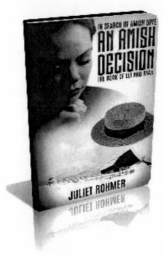

Thank you,

Juliet Rohmer

APPENDIX - GLOSSARY

Ach - Oh

Bruder - Brother

Bobli - Baby

Daed - Father

Danka - Thank you

Dat - Term used for grandfather

Englischer - Anyone who is not English.

Fraa - Wife

Grossmammi - Term used for grandmother.

Gott - God

Gut - God

Haus - house

Ja - Yes

Kapp - Cap (prayer cap)

Kaffee - Coffee

Kinner - Children

Kins-kind - Grandchildren

Mam - Term for one's mother.

Mann - Man

Mansleit - Men Folk

Ordnung - The agreed upon rules for living.

Rumspringa - The running around years

Sveshtah - Sister